Un-Break My Heart

CHERYL BARTON

Published by CRBarton Productions, LLC

CRBarton Productions, LLC
P.O. Box 962
Reisterstown, Maryland 21136
www.crbarton.com

Ordering Information:
Quantity sales. Special discounts are available on quantity purchases by corporations, associations, and others. For details, contact the publisher at the address above.

Orders by U.S. trade bookstores and wholesalers.
Please contact prez@crbarton.com

Cover Design: SelfPubBookCovers.com/DesignsbyDanielle

To my family, friends and fans who love reading and experiencing love, I want to thank you for your support and your friendship!

I am because you read - *Cheryl*

Connect with me:

Visit my website at www.CherylBarton.net
Twitter – @Author Cheryl Barton
Instagram – Author Cheryl Barton
Facebook - Author Cheryl Barton
Email – Cheryl@CherylBarton.net
Blog - https://mswriterinmd.wordpress.com/

About Un-Break My Heart

Mackenzie Ellis suffered a loss so great, she never thought she'd fall in love again, especially with someone close to her.

Travis Blackwell, III never dreamed of crossing the line with Mackenzie until his heart would no longer allow him to deny the love he has for her and the passion he wants to share with her knowing that he is the key to mending her broken heart.

OTHER ROMANCE NOVELS BY CHERYL BARTON

Bachelor Series

Bachelor Not For Sale
A Designed Affair
A Perfect Combination
Love at Last – Coming 2016

Amorous Occupations Series

The Artist
The Bookkeeper
The Chef
The Dancer
The Electrician
The Flight Attendant – Coming 2016

Inspirational Romance

Down, But Not Out: Breaking Chains

The McIntyre's Series

Xavier's Plan – Coming 2016
Spence's Challenge – Coming 2016

Stand Alone Romance Novels

Holly For Christmas
Second Chances: Three Valentine Novellas
Bossy – Coming 2016
Advantage, Love – Coming 2016

1

Dr. Mackenzie Ellis smiled and greeted everyone she passed along the halls of Sinnow Memorial Hospital, excited that the workday was coming to an end for her. Her exuberance wasn't solely about leaving the hospital where she worked as a pediatric surgeon, a job she loved, but it was more about the exciting plans she'd been hatching for days.

To her there was a time for work and then there was a time for everything else and that everything else is why she walked with an extra zest in her step.

More than working, time spent with her military husband, Kyle, was the most important part of her life. She was delighted that after four months of not seeing him, he was coming home for a few months. At thirty-three, she was ready to plan more for them than just fleeting moments as passing shadows when he had time to come home for a quick visit or if she was able to carve out time to fly to a destination where they could have a few days to be together. This visit was going to be the most exciting visit ever and she could barely contain the news she had to share with him.

"Dr. Ellis, I thought you were gone by now."

Mackenzie turned when she heard the voice of the head nurse on duty who also happened to be her best friend, Ava. She smirked knowing that Ava was trying to be snarky calling her doctor Ellis instead of just calling her Kenzie as she always did.

"I've been trying to get out of here for the past two hours and every time I think this hospital is about to set me free, I get pulled back in. You know how things can be when word gets out that a doctor is leaving for vacation."

She turned in the direction of footsteps heading her way and ducked behind the nurse's station to hide from anyone else who could ask a question that would cause her to stay even longer.

Four months may not seem long to a military family, but it seemed like an eternity for her since his last visit lasted a mere twenty-four hours. Before that visit, Kyle had been gone for almost a year, something she'd gotten accustomed to being married to a Navy SEAL.

Kyle's career kept them apart often, but she knew what she was in for when she'd met and then married him five years ago.

"I swear, one day I hope my best friend learns the art of saying no and thinking of herself for once in her life. I know you have a penchant for thinking of everyone else first, especially your patients, but you know this place will be okay if you take a few weeks off to get reacquainted with that handsome husband of yours."

"Yes and finally, I'll have him all to myself for more than a day."

Kyle had been on some top secret assignment for the past few months and they'd had no contact other than a cryptic voicemail message he'd left her a month ago telling her he missed her, loved her and would be home to see her in a month. She couldn't wait to hit him with one of her hot, hot kisses the moment he walked through the door.

"Kenzie, why are you still here?"

Mackenzie jumped up from the chair she'd plopped in providing her a little bit of privacy from the masses. Apparently that didn't include Carmen, her sister-in-law who also worked at the hospital as a physical therapist. She whipped her head around to once again explain herself.

"Like I just told Ava, I'm leaving right now," she said, reaching for the chart of one last patient she wanted to check on. Before she could get her hands on it, Carmen snatched it up.

"Oh, no you don't. Leave now before my brother gets home in a few days and wonders why you're so tired. How are the homecoming plans coming along?"

Mackenzie smiled a sexy, girlish grin at the thought of everything she had planned for Kyle when he returned.

"Kyle won't know what hit him and I get goosebumps every time I think of what his reaction is going to be when he hears he's going to be a father in five months."

She smiled as she rubbed her hand across her growing belly.

Mackenzie remembered the day the doctor confirmed what she already knew, which was that her dream of becoming a mother was finally coming true. She and Kyle knew when they married that they wanted to have children, but Kyle didn't want to start their family until he'd served his time with the SEALs, ended his twenty-year career with the military and took on a new career that kept him away from home a lot less often. She was looking forward to having lots of babies with him, starting with the one she was carrying.

She had been surprised at how quickly she'd gotten pregnant after putting her birth control aside right before his last visit home. After being home for one day, which they'd managed to spend in bed the entire time, a few weeks after he'd left to go on his mission, she discovered she was pregnant. She thought about sending him an email to tell him, but instead opted for an in-person surprise when he'd called to say he was finally getting more than a few days off to come spend some time with her. She held on to her secret and started planning a cute way of telling him by baking some of his favorite treats with one being in the shape of a baby onesie.

"My brother is going to be a great father," Carmen

said with enthusiasm at finally becoming an aunt.

"The last time he was home, we talked about babies and he was happy that we were going to finally start trying at the end of this year when his tour was finally up. He'll be shocked to know it happened quicker than either of us thought it would. That brother of yours is about to be thirty-eight and he said he wanted to be a father before he turned forty and it looks like he's getting his wish."

"Well, I'm sure he'll keep you hemmed up for the next few weeks after he gets home so whenever you come up for air, call me and tell me all about his reaction to hearing about the baby," Ava said.

"Trust me when I say it's Kyle who will need to come up for air. I can't tell you how much I have missed that man and to know that soon, he'll be done with the SEALs and finally going into business with Trey and the other guys. I know he'll still be busy all the time, but at least it won't be for months at a time like it has been since we met and he'll be right here in town with me going to bed together at night and waking up together every morning. We've both been working hard these past few years and saving all of our money and I can't wait to having this baby. I told you my plan is to spend a few years doing nothing, but being a wife and mother."

"So you're really going to do it? You're going to take a leave of absence for a few years to stay home with the baby?"

Mackenzie shook her head with an affirmative,

happy that she would have the opportunity to do that. It had been the plan all along.

"Yes and even if I were to second guess that decision, Kyle would overrule me. He told me that we've been so focused on our careers that when the time came for babies, that's all he wanted me to focus on and I'm more than ready."

"Good for you and now that we've chatted longer than we should have, get out of here and start your vacation," Carmen said, pushing Mackenzie toward the exit.

"Carmen is right and don't you dare stop to talk to anyone on your way out that may distract you and rope you into taking a look at another patient."

Mackenzie exhaled and moved past them in the direction of the elevator. She was excited for the time off and knew when she returned, she would be wrapping things up so that as soon as the baby is born, she wouldn't have any loose ends. She did agree to do some consulting work from home and Kyle was okay with her doing that as long as it wouldn't take her away from the baby and it could be done on her own schedule. The hospital agreed, not wanting to lose her completely as their chief of pediatric surgery, so they figured keeping her around in a consulting capacity would keep their hospital as one of the top in the country for surgical procedures on infants.

"I'll talk to you both sometime tomorrow and Carmen, tell your mom I promise to send Kyle over the moment he gets home before he and I hibernate," she jibed.

Mackenzie got in the waiting elevator, wiggled her fingers saying goodbye just as the elevator doors closed. Nothing was going to keep her away from the man she loved more than anything.

When the elevator reached her car level, she practically skipped to her car, feeling giddy like a little child waiting for Santa on Christmas morning. She had a few days to get her plans in place for an over the top welcome home for Kyle and more than anything, she couldn't wait for him to hear her great news. She first had to find a way to hide her growing belly until her plan for surprising him with the news was in place. Their lives were about to change and no one in the world was as happy at this very moment as she was. Her Kyle was coming home!

2

Travis Blackwell exhaled after his all day debriefing session at the Pentagon in Washington, D.C. His last assignment had been as top secret as they come and since he was preparing for his exit from the military in a few short months, he knew the first of many of these were coming up. At a young age, he'd decided to make a career in the military and loved the rush of every assignment. For the first time in his life, he was happy to be leaving it behind in order to find a life that wasn't as mobile as his.

The military had afforded him the opportunity to see more of the world than he even knew existed. The last nineteen or so years had been hard on him and at thirty-eight, it was time for him to find a little more stability in his life. He knew he would never be able to leave his life as a Navy SEAL in his past forever, especially since he and his best friend Kyle and a few of their friends were planning to start a private security and investigations business. Even though he would still be involved in some of the worst situations in the world in their new line of business, he was hoping to find happiness and contentment like Kyle had found when he met and fell in love with Mackenzie. He hadn't been as lucky and perhaps it was because he had a little more of his father in him than he knew or was willing to acknowledge.

His father, Travis Blackwell, Jr., was the epitome of a poppa who was a rolling stone. It was because he was named after his father that he resorted to using Trey, since he was the third, instead of people calling him Travis. All of his memories of his father were not good ones. There was even talk that there were several other children he fathered around California. From what he had been told by his mother, he had siblings he didn't know he had until he was an adult. Though he had yet to meet them, in his line of work, one of the things he planned to focus on was finding as many of them as he could. His mother thought there were five in total and none of them had the same mother so tracking them down could be hard, but he was serious about finding them.

His father had been a man who never stayed in one place for any long stretch of time. He knew that when his parents met, they'd had a whirlwind affair that led to a quick marriage and a few months later, he was born. He loved his father, but when he'd walked out on them when Trey was ten years old and never looked back, he harbored hatred for him, especially since they carried the same name.

His father may have left them, but he didn't leave Monterey, California where they lived. He'd see him around town, but the close bond he thought they were developing when he was little was nonexistent and so he started avoiding running into him whenever he could.

As he got older and reached high school, he saw his father less and less and that was okay with him since he hated the man for not doing his part as a father and leaving his mother to work two jobs to support the two of them. He was all the example Trey had of a father until he met Kyle in his freshman year of high school and his family had taken to him as if he was one of their own.

Kyle's father, David Ellis, was the greatest man he'd ever known. He was there for him just as he was for his own son and that's something he would always be grateful to the Ellis family for.

He and Kyle had excelled in high school athletics and though he knew he would never look out and see his own father in the stands cheering him on, he would look up into the stands and see Kyle's father not just cheering Kyle on, but him as well.

When he and Kyle made the decision to join the military together after graduating high school, his own mother moved to Florida to be closer to other family members. He decided to stay in Monterey and make that his permanent home, that place to always come back to when he could get time away from the military. Once he'd signed up, he never saw his father again.

He had been five years in when he received word that his father had passed away. By the time he'd gotten word, a cousin had already buried his father and his mother had decided not to attend the funeral services. He wasn't sad for the loss because he didn't really know his father, but he was sad that they never got the chance to make things right. He finally learned to move on beyond the hurt and dive head first into his life as a Navy SEAL.

Now almost twenty years after signing up, he and Kyle were once again making a decision that impacted them both which was to leave the military and start a private security and investigations business with a few other pals who were also making the transition back to civilian life.

He admired his best friend because he had the one thing that Trey didn't realize was missing in his own life until he made the decision to retire from the military. While Kyle was leaving and going back to a life with Mackenzie, Trey realized he didn't have that. He didn't know that he wanted it until recently. Thinking again about his father, he was more like him than he wanted to be, going from one woman to the next just for sexual gratification, but nothing long-lasting. His longest relationship lasted as long as he was on leave in any given town or country and then it was on to a new assignment and on his next break, he'd be on another woman, literally. That was fine for the kind of life he lived, but now that he was leaving that life behind, he had his empty house to go back to and only Kyle knew and understood what he was going through.

Kyle had once told him that the greatest day in his life was the day he'd met Mackenzie when he'd gone home for a visit some years back. One day while on leave about six or seven years ago, he decided to surprise his sister at the hospital where she worked. When he walked up to surprise her, his eyes locked with a cute resident, Mackenzie Albright, and any thoughts of other women were non-existent. He had been home on a two week stint and in that time, he and Mackenzie were inseparable and had fallen in love.

Kyle was currently away on a mission that didn't include him and it bothered him. They often didn't end up in the same place when it came to missions, but something about the mission Kyle was on didn't sit well with him. He knew how dangerous it was and he preferred to be the one having his friend's back in the kind of situation he knew Kyle was in.

He felt a responsibility for making sure every time Kyle went out on a mission, that he returned and even more so now that he was married and looking forward to starting a family with Mackenzie soon.

He hated the Kyle that turned into a puppy in love because he used the fact that he was no longer going from woman to woman to tell him that he needed to stop sleeping around and find a woman that he could fall in love with and start a life that involves love, a wife and hopefully a house full of kids. Kids were something Trey never thought he'd want or have, but the more Kyle talked about the plans he has once he leaves the military, the more he began seeing that kind of life for himself. For now, he looked forward to loving and spoiling the kids he knew Kyle wanted with Mackenzie.

Being an only child of his mother, he never had brothers and sisters around other than his closeness with Kyle and his sister Carmen. He had his mother, whom he was thankful for, but the thought of leaving service and going back to having a countless number of women in his bed on lonely nights was not the answer. He wanted to be around family and like Kyle, he hoped to one day have a family of his own. The reality was he was leaving the life he'd known for almost twenty years and going home to no one.

Walking back to his rental car after leaving the Pentagon, he heard his name being called. He turned to see a naval officer that he'd been friends with over the years. They hadn't stayed in close contact, but Trey considered him a good friend.

"What's happening Trey?"

"Hey Mike! Nothing much on my end. Just another long day of briefings and thankfully, I get a reprieve tomorrow. What's happening with you?"

"I hear that. I'm heading over to the Pentagon for a meeting and I thought that was you. So you're really going to do it huh? You're finally leaving?"

"Yeah, I am and believe me I thought it over a million times, but my decision hasn't changed. It's time for me to finally do something different."

"What does a SEAL do when he's no longer a SEAL?" Mike asked curiously.

"I don't know, but I'm looking forward to finding out."

He and the guys he was planning on going into business with hadn't told a lot of people of their post military plans and he didn't want to get into a long discussion about it. They've had things going on in the background for almost a year and until it's up and running, he was planning to stay closed mouth about it.

"I'm sure you have many women to catch up with in several cities around the world. I heard about your escapades," Mike said, facetiously.

Trey laughed.

"Don't believe everything you hear," he replied. "Make sure you stay in touch and maybe we can grab a few the next time you're in Cali.

"You got it," Mike said before turning and walking way.

Trey had just reached out to open the door to the car when his cell phone rang. He didn't recognize the number and contemplated not answering. He was in dire need of some down time and was hoping to get it, uninterrupted. When it stopped ringing, he let it roll to voicemail and got in the car. He sat for a few minutes and his phone rang again with that same number. He was about to answer it when he noticed a lot of activity outside the window of the car. A few people in uniform either broke out into a run or a swift walk. He wondered what the emergency was.

Again, his phone chimed and this time he answered it and never got out words of greeting.

"Trey, I need you back here on the double. Are you done in DC? If so, you need to be on the first flight out. There is a military transport ready to bring you here so drop everything and get moving."

Trey knew where "here" was, but he didn't know why. Looking around again, something was definitely wrong and it had to be bad.

"Sir, can you tell me anything about what's going on," he said as he put his car in gear and sped off.

He received silence and knew it must be bad.

"Sir?" he asked again. "What's going on? I can tell it's serious because here at the Pentagon, there seems to be an uptake in activity."

"It is bad," he heard as his commander's voice went deeper and more sullen.

"How bad is bad?" he asked and then his thoughts turned to Kyle and his heart dropped.

"The worse it could be Trey which is why I need you here."

"Kyle?" he asked, holding his breath hoping to hear the word, 'no'. Instead of hearing that one word in response, he was met with silence and he knew. He didn't say his friend's name again.

"How bad is the situation?"

"I can't do this over the phone Trey, you know that. Your line isn't secure."

He could feel himself getting angry being left with

the unknown. He needed to know and he needed to know now.

"Sir, I mean no disrespect, but at this moment, I don't give a damn about secure lines. This is Kyle we're talking about and I need to know what I'm up against. How bad is he?" he asked.

There was a long break that was probably only a few seconds, but seemed like a lifetime of waiting for an answer.

"He's gone Trey. He and another member of the team were killed trying to protect a family that got caught in the line of fire."

Trey slammed on his breaks not sure he understood what he'd just heard. Did he just hear that his best friend had been killed? Kyle, like him, had eight or nine months left to serve and this is not how he was supposed to go out.

"Trey? I know this is a lot, but I need you to focus and get here. I'm rounding up the rest of your team as soon as I know you're good and on your way. I know you may need time to process this, but I can't give you that. I didn't want you hearing about it before I had a chance to talk to you."

"On my way," he responded and hung up.

Trey sat in his car in the middle of traffic and stared out of the front window, stunned. He wanted to drive off after hearing cars behind him honking for him to get out of the way, but he couldn't move. He needed to take a few minutes to wrap his mind around what he'd just heard. He wanted to explode, but he couldn't. He needed to get to the transport to find out what happened that now snatched Kyle from their lives; the lives of his parents, sister and especially the love of his life Mackenzie.

"Oh no," he thought and then said out loud.

"Mackenzie," was all he said before flooring the gas pedal and making his way to the airport.

3

"Mom, I'm feeling fine and I promise I'm not doing too much. This is the first time I'm going to see Kyle in four months and I want to make the most of the month that he'll be here. This is his last tour and then we'll finally get to have the life we've planned for and dreamed about. I know you think I'm overdoing it, but I'm not. I'm taking it easy and the doctor said the pregnancy is going well and that there are no issues, so please stop worrying."

"How much longer are you going to work at the hospital?"

"I actually started my month long vacation yesterday and I'm planning to work until the baby is born. The plan is that I'm going to stay at home with the baby, according to Kyle, as long as I want to and just in case we want to have a second baby not long after this one, I may be out indefinitely. I am planning to work as a consultant on special cases at the hospital which is something I can do from home, so I'll still be connected to the hospital and the work that I love."

"I'm so excited about the baby and glad that you'll be able to stay home and enjoy it. You and Kyle have planned well for this and I can't wait until you tell him about the baby. He's going to be overjoyed and probably walking around banging on his chest like Tarzan," her mother laughed loudly.

Mackenzie herself laughed because her mother knew Kyle well. She loved him as if he were her son instead of her son-in-law. She wished her parents lived closer to her in Monterey. They lived on the other side of the country in Virginia where they moved many years ago when her father accepted a promotion within his company.

"This baby is what Kyle and I have been talking about for a while now and we were planning to start working on it after he finally finished his service, but I went off the pill early thinking it would take me a while to get pregnant and it happened during that one day the last time he was home. I'm ready for him to get here. Believe me I'm not doing too much."

"Okay, I'm going to let you get back to what you were doing. I wanted to call and check on you before your father and I left for our cruise. We leave out in two days so I will talk to you when we return. Make sure you give Kyle a big hug and kiss from me and tell him we'll see him soon. Love you Kenzie."

"I love you too Mom and tell Dad I said hello."

Mackenzie hung up and turned back around to finish unpacking the items she'd picked up from the store. She knew Kyle loved getting out of his military gear while home so she went out and picked up pairs of his favorite designer jeans and shirts, extra toiletries and of course her favorite thing she loved seeing him in, boxer briefs.

She grabbed her last load of clothes to wash and headed down to the kitchen to finish the laundry and start doing some of her baking. In two more days, Kyle would be walking through the door and she would begin the first of many glorious days with him until he had to return to duty. This last mission he was assigned to was top secret and having any kind of contact with him while he was gone was impossible, but she knew that would soon be over. She thought that he would have called or emailed her by now to let her know that he was back on United States soil. She shook it off and assumed he wanted to take care of loose ends so that he could get home as soon as possible.

Mackenzie turned on some music and danced around to the slow tunes of Earth, Wind & Fire and hadn't noticed that someone was standing at her door until she turned and was startled by their sudden appearance.

It took her a few seconds to realize the person standing at the door was Trey. He was impeccably clad in his service dress blue uniform which was out of character for a casual visit.

Before she could make her way to the door, he opened it and removed his hat. She looked beyond him wondering when Kyle would pop out assuming he was with him. After a few seconds, not only did Kyle not reveal himself, but Trey hadn't smiled as he usually did when she saw him. The look on his face made her pause when he tried hard to avoid a direct stare into her eyes. Where she had begun walking toward him she halted aware that something was wrong. Her heart nearly stopped beating when there was movement behind Trey as he entered the house.

Where she thought Kyle would enter, there were two other men also in their service dress blues coming into the house behind him. Doubt, fear and confusion overwhelmed her. The reason most obvious to her of why they would be in her house seemed like a scene out of a movie. Mackenzie looked from Trey to the two men and then back to Trey whose expression had turned grave.

She couldn't move when suddenly her feet felt like lead. The look on Trey's face said it all and when he couldn't speak or say a word, she knew it couldn't be good news. Her eyes never left his face and she could read the signs of dread filling his expression and in the professional demeanor of his stance that he wasn't making a social call. Something had happened to Kyle and from the look of things, it was the worse news possible.

"Mrs. Kyle Ellis, my name is..."

Before one of the men who had accompanied Trey

could finish what he was about to say, Mackenzie put up her hand to signal him to stop. Even while she did so, her eyes still remained on Trey who had yet to speak.

"Mrs. Ellis," the other man said.

"Shut up," she said in a quiet, but stern voice that she never knew she had.

"Mrs. Ellis," the first guy tried again.

"I said shut up," she said again, this time through gritted teeth.

"Trey?"

From the look on his face, she could see that he was holding back saying anything because if he did, she knew he feared he too would break down and the more she looked at him the more she knew what he came to tell her and she wanted him to do it. If he were going to bring her bad news then she needed him to do it and not two strangers.

"Trey? Say it. You have to say it. I don't want to hear from anyone, but you at this moment and you have to say it," she pleaded.

Trey looked at her and then looked away.

"Look at me Trey," she said austerely.

Trey turned his eyes back to hers and his heart dropped at the sight of her standing before him waiting for bad news to drop.

"Kenzie, let these men do their job. I'm here because I begged to be allowed to come so that you would have someone here who was familiar to you."

She spoke in an even harsher tone on the brink of

tears that were already pooling in her eyes; she already knew.

"I don't want to hear a damn thing from either one of them," she said, ready to collapse in a fit of emotional turmoil.

Trey looked at both men and without saying a word, they stepped back to allow him to handle the situation. He then turned his attention back to Kenzie and just before he was about to bring her the worse possible news, he noticed something different about her. She was pregnant, something he was sure Kyle had not known because if he had, Trey would have been the first person he would have told. Now he knew that the news he had to bring her was about to be harder than he originally thought it would be, if that were possible. He had a job to do and he needed to do it so that he could be here for her in the aftermath.

"Kenzie, why don't you have a seat," he said looking from her face to her stomach.

Mackenzie followed his gaze and realized he was able to see that she was pregnant.

"Say it Trey. Say what you came to say," she said already crying unable to hold back the tears that at first were only threatening to fall.

Trey walked closer to her and Mackenzie reached out her hand to stop him as wave after wave of terror overtook her. Her legs began to give out as she reached for something to steady herself. She felt sick to her stomach as her heart raced and her head began to spin. In between cries of horror and anxiety she tried to stay focused on what he came to do.

"Kenzie, please sit down."

"Dammit Trey, stop it. Just say it, right now; just say it," she screamed with all of her might.

Trey mustered up every bit of strength he had and looking his best friend's wife in the eyes, he told her.

"He's gone Kenzie. Kyle was killed two days ago while on a mission. I'm sorry to have to tell you this, but I couldn't let anyone else come here, but me."

Before he could get out another word, Mackenzie let out a scream that Trey knew could have been heard by everyone in the neighborhood. Nothing could compare to the devastation he was feeling watching her go through the worse pain of her life. When he noticed she was about to drop to the floor, he reached for her to break her fall and to protect the baby.

The hurt he'd felt since finding out his friend had been killed had resurfaced again, twenty-fold as he watched Kenzie cry for the man who had been her everything for what seemed an eternity. He tried to hold her as her body heaved from the tears and screams and before he knew what he was doing, he was crying just as hard as she was. He hadn't had time to grieve over Kyle's death because his first thought was of Kyle's family, especially Mackenzie. He knew that right now, Kyle's parents were going through the same fit of emotions that Mackenzie was going through since two officers had been dispatched to tell them at the same time that he and the other two officers were sent to tell Mackenzie.

"No!" Mackenzie screamed over and over while gripping her stomach.

Trey tried to hold on as tight as he could until he felt her pulling away from him.

"How could you let this happen to him Trey? Wha.., what happened to him? Why is Kyle dead?" she stuttered out through screams and tremors.

"I'm sorry Kenzie. I'm so sorry I wasn't there to save him. He died trying to save a woman and her children."

"I don't care about another woman and her children when my husband is dead. You were supposed to have his back and make sure that he always came home to me, always!"

"Kenzie, I'm sorry and I swear if I could trade places with him, I would."

Mackenzie didn't know if she had any tears left in her body, but what she did have plenty of was rage. She turned her attention full on to him.

"If you could trade places with him, I would let you, but right now, I can't look at you. I can't look at any of you, so please take your men and get out of my house," she cried.

Trey pulled himself together and tried to think clearly in order to help Mackenzie get through the shock of hearing that Kyle had been killed.

"Mackenzie, I can't leave you here like this. Let me take you to Kyle's parents' house so that you're not alone. Do you need a doctor? I'm concerned about the baby. Please, just let me help you." he begged.

Mackenzie pulled herself from Trey's embrace as she

looked at him with as much hatred for him as she would have for the person who took Kyle's life. To her, Trey was the enemy and she couldn't be around him.

"I don't want or need your help Trey, but what I do need is for you and your men to get out of my house right now. You did what you came to do and right now I need to be alone."

"I'm not just military here to bring you bad news; I'm Kyle's best friend and I know that he would want me to make sure you're okay before I leave you here all alone."

"Kyle is dead Trey. Isn't that what you just told me? I can't look at you and not relive those words coming out of your mouth over and over again. Kyle isn't going to walk through that door any minute to tell me he loves me. You're worried about me and this baby? Then be more worried about the fact that you and this military just made me a widow and my child has no father, so the last thing I want right now is any of you in my house. Now I'm going to say it again; friend or not, get out! Get out right now!" she shouted.

Trey knew she was speaking out of hurt and despair and he accepted that. He'd just given her awful news and she had a right to lash out at the world.

"Tell me what I can do to help you, but please don't ask me to leave you here. I'll do anything I can to help you get through this," Trey said somberly.

"Can you bring Kyle back? Can you un-break my heart right now because it's hurting with a pain I've never experienced before? I feel like my heart is literally burning in my chest. Can you fix that or turn the clock back to a time where we wouldn't need to have this conversation?"

Trey was about to plead with her again to let him stay when he heard the front door and saw Carmen running through it with tears streaming down her face.

As soon as Mackenzie laid eyes on Carmen, her crying spell returned as she turned her attention from Trey and embraced her sister-in-law and they cried together. As much as Trey wanted to stay and console them, he knew that as long as he stood in her house in his uniform, she would never see him as just Trey, but as a member of the military that had now taken her husband's life. Again, he understood her anger.

"I'm sorry Mackenzie. If you need anything, please call me and I'll be right here."

Trey turned with the other two officers and left the house closing the door behind him. He got in the back seat of the car and as they drove off, he did something he would only do in the darkened back seat of the car with tinted windows blocking him from anyone outside looking in; he cried for his best friend, a man he would gladly have given his life for. He didn't know how Mackenzie would survive Kyle's loss and he started questioning whether he would.

4

Mackenzie laid in bed for the third day in a row, still not able to pull herself up to get back to her life. Kyle's funeral had taken place a week ago and after family and friends had returned back their lives, she was enjoying the peace and tranquility of being alone to grieve her broken heart. Her life would never be the same again and though people tried to be nice, she longed for quiet time to figure out how she was going to live without her Kyle. She was about to doze off to sleep again when her bedroom door opened and in walked her mother. Her parents had flown out immediately after she called and gave them the news and they'd stayed with her since then.

"Kenzie, tell me you're not going to spend another full day in this bed. You have to get up sweetheart and stay active. I know all you want to do is stay in this bed and think about Kyle, but I'm concerned that you're not getting any better."

Mackenzie sat up and turned to her mother.

"Mom, I'm fine and I don't want you worrying about me. There had been so many people in and out of here for the past few weeks since Kyle died and now I feel like I can rest quietly. I promise you I'm doing okay."

"Are you sure you're feeling okay? What about the baby? You know babies can sense stress and pain and though I know you've been eating, I want to be sure you're moving around and not wallowing in pity every day. That's not healthy for the baby or for you. Your father told me if I couldn't get you to come downstairs with me, he was going to come, pick you up and bring you downstairs even if he had to carry you and you know he will. You haven't been out of here in days."

Mackenzie smiled knowing that her father would follow through on his promise. She was glad they'd stayed the extra time after the funeral to help her out. They would have to get back to their life in Virginia soon and her mother would not leave unless she knew that they could leave her alone.

She was finally coming to terms with Kyle's death, accepting that he was never coming back to her and because she had a life growing inside of her which was a symbol of the love they shared, she needed to get herself together and rejoin the living.

"Okay, there is no need for Dad to get all dramatic. I'm getting up right now and I'll be down right after I get a shower and put on some clothes. How is that?"

she said smiling and moving to get out of bed.

"Your father will be happy to see you come down. Kyle's father is downstairs with him and they've both been worried to death about you. I'll let you get your shower and I'll go down to get lunch started."

Mackenzie watched as her mother paused before going back out of the bedroom door.

"What is it Mom?"

"Trey has been by here every day asking about you and wanting to see you. I've given him one excuse after another, but I'm afraid I don't have any more to give if he comes by again. He has to leave tomorrow and I know he wants to see you before he does. Are you still not ready to talk to him?"

Hearing Trey's name made her angry all over again. He'd been calling and texting her since the funeral. She'd been unable to say more than hello to him.

"I can't talk to him right now Mom. There is still too much hurt there and every time I see him, all I can think about is the fact that Kyle is gone and I can't handle that. I need him to give me some time."

"I know dear, but he leaves tomorrow and won't be back for a few weeks."

"He saw me at the funeral and here at the house after the funeral so he knows I'm okay. He doesn't need to talk to me to know that."

"It's not Trey's fault that Kyle died. He died doing what he had pledged his life to do and if Trey could have done anything to prevent what happened, he would have and you know that. He was Kyle's best friend and I know that Kyle would want Trey to look after you as much as he could since he can't be here himself to do that."

"Kyle should be here to look after me. I didn't even get a chance to tell him he was going to be a father. He'll never get the chance to see his daughter's face and love her the way I know he would. I know Trey means well, but I can't handle the steady reminder by seeing him right now. I just need a moment and maybe he should just go back and do what he needs to do and he can check on me when he returns in a few weeks. Right now isn't a good time."

Mackenzie went to her closet to grab some clothes to put on after her shower as she heard her mother close the bedroom door. She looked at herself in the mirror and noticed how much bigger her stomach had gotten over the past month. Her heart broke a little more each time realization set in that she would be raising their child alone.

No woman wanted to do that and she was no exception. Her plan was to have this baby and many others and she and Kyle would grow old together one day enjoying their grandchildren. What was she going to do now? Everything they'd had planned was now a dream, buried with Kyle.

She wondered what life would be like for her and her little girl who she planned to name, Kylie. Kylie would only get to hear about and not experience the love her father would have had for her. There will always be that empty spot in their lives where he was supposed to be to love and take care of them.

Before meeting Kyle, Mackenzie never knew being in love could be so wonderful. She'd met Kyle at a time when she was about to give up on falling in love. She'd gone through what most women go through moving from one relationship to the next and not coming across that one person that would leave her speechless, but that's exactly what happened the minute she and Kyle locked eyes. He gave her a look that was so intense, if she could read it aloud, she would think that he'd just told her that she was his and there was nothing she could do about it. From that day forward, they were meant to be together.

Their romance was something out of a fairytale that a woman believes comes once in a lifetime. He had been home visiting his family and fate had intervened because she was scheduled to be off that day and if she hadn't agreed to fill in for another resident, she would have missed locking eyes with Kyle and all of his gorgeousness.

He never missed a chance to tell her how beautiful she was and how much he loved her. When he was away for long, extended periods of time, he would send her letters and emails letting her know how much he missed her and how she was the bright spot of his day in the dreary and dreadful world he lived in. They had a love that she read about in romance novels and it was supposed to last forever.

Mackenzie knew she'd love him forever, but she wanted him here with her so that he could love her forever. Those dreams of being together forever have now been shattered along with her heart. She knew that as long as she lived, she would never love another man the way she loved him and her heart would forever be broken into a million little pieces.

Ava had come by to see her a few times and they'd talked about love and how heart wrenching it could be when someone you love with everything in you is snatched away. Ava had tried convincing her that love was not meant to happen only once in a lifetime and though she knew how intense their love was, one day in the future, when she was ready, she hoped that she'd find it in her heart to love again, knowing that Kyle would want her to.

Love again? After what she had with Kyle, she didn't see that happening for her again. It was too soon for her to even be thinking in terms of another love, but she knew that Ava was trying to get her to see that Kyle wouldn't want her living a life without the kind of love they shared. Ava made it clear that yes, she should mourn and miss Kyle and go through all the stages of grieving for him, but she wouldn't be a friend if she allowed her to never move on.

No, she would never, ever love like that again because no man would care about her the way he did or make her feel like he lived and loved just for the love they shared. That kind of love only came around once in a lifetime and Kyle was hers.

She looked forward to her life with Kylie and she knew having her family around was exactly what she needed, but love wasn't in the cards for her ever again. As far as she was concerned, it died the day that Kyle had and no way could the pieces of her broken heart ever be put back together again.

**

Trey tried calling Mackenzie once again before his flight. He hadn't seen her since the days following Kyle's funeral and though he'd tried calling her a few times, she had yet to pick up the phone. He didn't know what else he could do to console and help her through this difficult time. As much as Kyle meant to her as her husband, he meant that much to him as his best friend. If the tables had been turned and their roles reversed, he knew that Kyle would look after his wife and soon to be born child if he had either.

His life wasn't filled with the love of a wife as Kyle's had been. He had made the military his bride and focused his time and attention to that. Kyle, on the other hand, though just as dedicated to the job as he was, felt his life was complete because he had Mackenzie and that he could return home knowing she'd always be there.

He was having just as much of a hard time coping with Kyle's loss as Mackenzie, though on a different level. He kept hoping day after day that Kyle being gone wasn't true and any minute his cell phone would vibrate with a text message joke from Kyle. Times when they were too far away for a phone conversation, Kyle had a tendency to send him corny jokes by text along with encouraging words from one brother to another when he knew that Trey was heading into a life or death situation.

His thoughts stayed on Mackenzie day in and day out as he tried to come up with a way to help her deal with the fact that Kyle was never coming home again. He knew that his death wasn't his fault, but he felt responsible just the same.

As he had done over the past several days, when Mackenzie didn't answer his call, he hung up without leaving a message. He didn't want to talk to her voicemail and he knew that she still could not face him in a one on one conversation. He'd tried several times, but each time, she'd find a way to excuse herself from his presence.

He put his phone away in his duffle bag as he continued to pack for his trip to the airport. He looked around his home and until today, it had always been a place he was proud of and now more than ever, he wanted to fill it with the love of a family that he could come home to. Kyle had been right during times when they would have brother heart to heart conversations and he would remind Trey that one day he would look around and find that he wasted a lot of years blaming his father for his lack of commitment to women and that when he found that one woman, he would have a whole new outlook on love and life.

He looked around and his place seemed empty and so did his life. Kyle's death opened up his eyes to what was missing and he hoped one day that he'd be able to find the kind of love that would make him want to be home and no place else.

For now, he had a big chapter in his life to close and a brand new one to start.

He looked forward to starting that business with his friends, a plan that he and Kyle were going to do together with a few others from the military who were looking to stay in the field, but opted for less dangerous situations.

Their idea to start a private security and investigations agency was a great idea. Each guy was bringing his own sort of expertise. Now with Kyle gone, that left him who was an expert marksman and a wiz when it came to surveillance. Then there was Ivan who was a professional at making himself blend in and then disappearing and moving around places without being seen. Dustin was the brains of the group having both military and business management expertise. He was also built like a linebacker and no one ever wanted to go up against him in anything. Lincoln was all about technology. He had been recruited for the military years ago because of his knack for hacking into highly classified agencies and they thought it best to bring him on board to help the United States as opposed to sending him to prison. The last member of their group was Calvin or Cal, as they called him, who had contacts all over the world and an expert in anything that dealt with explosives.

They agreed to continue with their plans, doing so to honor Kyle. Prior to Kyle's death, they had decided on a name for the business, calling it, Game Changers

Security and Investigations. They would be operating as private contractors continuing to do what they had been doing while in the military, but doing things in their own way.

Kyle's absence was like a loud siren that couldn't be silenced. Everything Trey saw and did made him think of his best friend and how his life had been cut short. The one small bit of peace he did have was because he knew that Ivan had done what he would have liked to have done and that was he was able to take out the shooter that had killed Kyle and that gave him a temporary sense of satisfaction. It didn't bring his friend back and it didn't keep him from grieving daily, but it helped him deal with it a little better.

Now if he could just get Mackenzie to talk to him, he felt that they could help each other get through the worst of their days missing Kyle. His flight was pulling out in an hour and he wouldn't have time to swing by her house again so he called her one last time and this time he was going to leave her a message and hoped that if she needed him, she would call him. He dialed her number and as usual, he got her voicemail.

"Mackenzie, it's me and I know I'm the last person you want to hear from right now, but I was concerned about you and wanted to check on you before I pulled out. I stopped by the house a few times and your mother said you needed your rest so I didn't push, but I hope you'll feel up to talking to me soon. I know you're hurting and your heart is broken, but I'm here for you. I also wanted to say congratulations again on the baby and I hear it's a girl. I'm sorry your plans of having this baby with Kyle and getting on with your lives was cut short, but if you need anything from me for you or the baby, I'm here. I will always be here for you both and I hope one day you'll let me in to be the friend I've always been to you. I'm leaving today, but I'll be back in a few weeks and hopefully by then, you'll be open to seeing me. Take care of yourself and that little baby and I hope to hear from you soon. Bye."

He tried not to dwell on it anymore as he hung up, grabbed his bag and left his house. He moved his truck into the garage next to his car and took a cab to the airport. Maybe what he needed was a few weeks away to gather his thoughts and start preparing for his life after the military. Kyle always told him he needed to take the time to focus more on his personal life and less on the military so that he one day could have more than an empty house to come to each day. That thought rang out more for him now than it ever had in the past. It was time for him to get his life together.

5

Mackenzie was all packed and ready to go. Her parents were returning to Virginia and she'd decided to go back with them until after the baby was born. She couldn't deal with being in Monterey where everyone wanted to tell her how sorry they were that Kyle had died sending her back down that spiral staircase again and again. She was trying to get her life back together and prepare for the birth of her daughter in a few months and though she had Kyle's family and all of her friends, she wanted to be around her family. When her parents asked her to come back with them, she hesitated at first and then decided to take them up on the offer because she could use the time away. Her doctor was concerned about what he was calling her slipping in to a depressive state and thought getting away from so many memories would help.

She never did return to work and now was planning to do so when Kylie was at least six months old, so going to Virginia for a while seemed like a good plan.

She would love nothing more than to continue with the plans that she and Kyle had for her to stay home with the baby, but now that he was gone, she needed to get back to life and her job would help ease her back into what her life needed to be about which was providing for her and the baby.

As she looked around for any last minute things she wanted to take, her thoughts turned to Trey. He had been the only person she had not talked to in the past two weeks and she knew he was scheduled to return to Monterey in a few days and she'd be in Virginia by then. She didn't know what to say to him at this point. Even though Kyle was on her mind every day, whenever she saw or thought of Trey, all she saw was the day he delivered her the news and she couldn't shake it. She hoped a little time away would help ease some of the hurt.

"Kenzie, are you ready to go?" her mother said walking past the bedroom.

"Yes, I'm ready. Tell Dad the last box of stuff for the baby is ready for the delivery man when he gets here."

"Great, we're ready to leave. Carmen is here and ready for any list minute instructions you have for her about the house. I'll send her up so that she can help you with any last minute packing."

Mackenzie nodded and moved around the room doing one last check to be sure she had everything. She turned around to see Carmen coming in the bedroom.

"I just walked by the baby's room and it looks so nice. Are you still going to have it painted? I can have someone take care of that while you're gone."

"That would be great. I wanted to get the furniture in it to see what it would look like, but yes, if you can have it painted with the colors I picked out, that would be a big help."

"I'm glad to see you're doing better these days."

She was coming along slowly, but her new reality was a little hard to embrace some days.

"I'm hanging in there. How are your parents doing? I was planning to stop by to see them today before I left, but I ran out of time."

"They're doing better," Carmen replied.

"I spoke with them a few days ago when they stopped by after hearing that I was going to Virginia for a while. I think they wanted to know that I was going to be coming back. This is my home and I'm planning on coming back to my life here. At this point, I can't say exactly when, but I know they have a big anniversary coming up in less than a year and I promise I will be here by the time that comes around. I wouldn't miss being a part of the festivities I know you're planning. If there is any part of that where I can help you by phone or email, let me know."

"I will and I'll let them know that you got off okay today. Just make sure you call us when you land and get settled in at your parent's home. Have you had a chance to talk to Trey lately?"

Mackenzie looked at Carmen and then looked away. She still wasn't sure she could talk to Trey without breaking down in a fit of body-racking tears.

"I haven't talked to him in weeks. I think he's coming home in a few days and then he has a few more months before he'll be out and back home for good. Have you talked to him?" she asked curious.

"He called the house a few times to check on the family and he asked about you and the baby and I told him you were both doing fine. Kenzie, what's the problem between you two? It can't be that you blame him for Kyle's death and I know he wants to help you heal so why won't you let him?"

Mackenzie wasn't surprised at how open and blunt Carmen was. She wasn't one to hold anything back.

"I don't know. I think it still has a lot to do with the day he delivered the news to me about Kyle. I know a conversation would turn to Kyle and I'm not ready to do that with him yet."

"He's feeling left out and I know I would feel that way if I were in his shoes. I hope you can see that he's trying to help. He misses Kyle as much as any of us and he needs us around just like you do and he feels that you cutting him out is because you blame him for not having Kyle's back. We know that's not true or at least I hope that's not true."

Mackenzie sat down feeling the weight of the guilt she carried around when she knew part of her wanted to blame him because he wasn't there to watch his back. Deep down she knew it wasn't fair putting such a burden on someone whom she knew would have given his own life to protect Kyle's.

"I'm sorry Carmen. I know Trey isn't responsible for what happened to Kyle and I think in my hurt I dished a lot of anger his way because he's here and Kyle isn't. I also know that he's only trying to help and I appreciate his desire to want to do that, but right now I can't handle seeing him. All I see when I do look at him is the day he walked into this house and brought me bad news. Then the day of the funeral, he was in those same dress blues and it all came flooding back to me again. I just need a little bit of a breather from him and everything military even if it's just for a little while. I'm not trying to cut him out of my life and I would never cut him out of the baby's life. I have a lot to get through and deal with and right now, Trey brings up memories I don't want to focus on. I promise you that I will call him."

"What do you want me to tell him when he gets home and finds that you've moved to Virginia?"

Mackenzie looked at her and smile when she caught that she'd said the word 'moved'.

She turned and swung her hips flippantly in Carmen's direction to lighten the conversation.

"I'm not *moving* to Virginia. I'm going for a visit just to get away and you know I'm planning on returning to the hospital, so that should tell you I'm returning. If he asks, tell him I'm visiting my parents in Virginia and that the baby and I are doing fine," she said rubbing her hand across her stomach.

"Only a few more months and I get to meet my niece," Carmen said with glee.

"She certainly is a busy one. She's active all day and night."

"Does your doctor have any worries?"

"None other than my moods and I told him I'm working on that. Usually in times like this, a doctor would prescribe something to help a grieving spouse relax and sleep, but because of the baby, he couldn't so he checks in often. He's already reached out to a doctor in Virginia that he trusts that'll deliver the baby. I'm going to be fine and so is the baby. I have my bad days as any woman in my position would, but I believe with time, it will get better."

"I'm glad to hear that and Trey will be happy to hear you're doing well. I think my mom talked to him yesterday and mentioned he'll be back sometime tomorrow. You couldn't wait a day or two to leave so huh?"

Mackenzie knew the timing looked suspect, but she wasn't leaving before he returned in order to avoid him. She felt the time was right and she was doing it before she changed her mind.

"Trust me when I tell you I will call him and I will apologize for how I've been acting, but I think Trey understands what I'm going through. He has always seemed like the patient type of person and I think once I'm ready, he will get the reassurance he needs to know that I'm doing fine."

"Okay, no more Trey talk then. We love you and we

all want to see you get through this. My niece will need you happy and smiling so that she won't sense that anything is wrong. I know that grieving can go on for years and years and I hope that it won't take you that long because my brother wouldn't want that. He would expect that you would take the time you need to mourn and then remember that he died doing what he was born to do."

"Yes he did and for that I'm a very proud of him, but I miss him so much. I never knew my heart would hurt this much and that's because I never dreamed of a time when he would not be here with me or at least returning to me."

"One day that hurt will ease up a little more and a little more and you'll feel like yourself again. One day you'll want to love again and you'll know when it's the right time to do that. I know it seems too new to talk about that, but that's a part of life. I loved my brother with everything that's in me, but he wouldn't want anything short of love and happiness for you in your future."

"I could never love anyone like I loved him."

"This is all new and it's okay to feel that way, but trust me when I tell you it will be okay if or when you do. We love you and life is too short to never have that kind of love again. One day when Kylie is in her forties, I'll give you permission to then fall in love again and you'll be what, in your seventies by then? I think that's a good time," Carmen laughed and moved when Mackenzie smiled and tried to push her.

"Funny Carmen. I love you too and I appreciate the love and support. Let's get the rest of this stuff into the car. Everything else is being shipped to arrive in a few days."

"It's good to see you smile."

Mackenzie felt good smiling.

"It feels good to smile again," she admitted.

6

The cab dropped Trey off at his house and instead of going inside, he instead opened the garage and got in his truck and headed straight for Mackenzie's house. He'd had no contact with her since Kyle's funeral and he wanted to see for himself that she was okay. He knew she had to be going through a lot emotionally and he still wanted her to know that he was here for her even if she continued to avoid him.

In the thirty minutes it took for him to drive out to her house, he thought through how he would handle the situation if she still didn't want to see him. Enough time had now passed to the point that they should be able to talk and heal together.

He pulled into her driveway right behind Carmen's car. After exiting, the front door of the house opened and Carmen launched herself into his arms.

"Trey, you're home!" she exclaimed.

"Hey Car! How is everyone?" he asked.

"Everyone is fine and doing well, but if you're here to see Kenzie, she's not here. She's in Virginia staying with her parents until the baby is born. If you had been here one day earlier, you would have caught her before she left."

The news stunned him that she'd pack up and leave.

"She just left?"

"Well, she didn't just leave. She needed to get away for a bit. Her parents had been here for a while and needed to return home and she decided to go with them after her doctor said it was okay for her to travel and he felt the change in scenery would help her. You still haven't talked to her?"

"I've tried calling her and she still won't take my calls or return any of the messages I left."

"Is your tour finally over?"

"Not exactly. I have some loose ends to wrap up for the next few months, but with all the briefings I'll have to do, it will take me the next few months to finish that up and then I'm officially discharged."

"You and other guys still plan on starting that investigations business you and Kyle were always talking about?"

"Yeah we are. In fact, I'm about to head over to the industrial park where the office will be. We purchased an old factory and warehouse that we're turning into our headquarters. I'll be here for a week and then off again, but the next time I return, I'll be back for good."

"I heard construction was going on over there, but

didn't know that it was you and your guys. There is no signage up yet."

"We've had some people handling things on this end while we each wrap up our business with our respective careers so that we can now focus on the business. The signage should be going up later this week. I approved it while I was away."

"Kyle was excited about ending his tour and going into business with all of you."

"I miss him too and we're planning to continue what we started because we know he would want us to."

"I can't wait to see what you guys do with that place. It's been sitting empty for a long time. What are you going to do with all of that space?"

"Well, between you and I, the investigations business can be tricky and dangerous so we plan to operate other businesses as a cover for the covert operations we plan to also run in helping to protect those in need. How are your parents doing?"

"They're fine. Kenzie is another story though and if it weren't for the baby, I think we would have opted for medicating her. That's why she felt like she needed to be close to her parents right now and going back with them was best for her. I haven't seen her smile in a long time and the excitement of getting away from here gave her something to focus on besides the fact that Kyle is gone. It's a good move for her, Trey."

"I understand that and I know," he acknowledged.

Trey remembered the day he brought her the news and the image of watching her crumble right before him still haunted him daily. It was the hardest thing he'd ever had to do and being in the military, he'd had his share of hard tasks.

"I know you're concerned about everyone else, but how have you been coping? You were just as close to Kyle as any of us and even more so since you served together."

"One day at a time. I wake up expecting a phone call from him telling me it was all a lie and he's not actually gone, but I know that's not going to happen. We were brothers and it feels like I lost a limb the day he died. If I'm feeling this way, I can't even begin to imagine what Mackenzie is going through, which is why coming here was my first stop after landing this morning."

"Sorry she's not reaching out to you or returning your calls, but it's not just you; she's been avoiding everyone including her friends at the hospital. I came by to get the mail and check on the house. I also started packing up Kyle's things from the house. I knew that she wasn't going to be able to do it. There were some things she wanted to keep, but others like his clothes, she asked me to donate to a shelter. At first she told me to leave everything where it was, but I told her that any healing she would do in Virginia would be for naught if she came back to her house and everything of Kyle's was still in it as if he were going to walk through the door at any moment. She finally agreed to let me pack it up, but I'm going to store everything and not get rid of it, unless you want any of it."

"No, go ahead and store it."

Trey looked around at the grass and the hedges.

"I'll come by later today and cut the grass, trim the hedges and cut back some of the tree branches. Anything else around here needs to be done?"

"I don't know what to do with his motorcycle. I don't really want to store it and I know she doesn't want it around since she never liked him riding it anyway."

"Leave that to me. I think it will be a nice addition to our office as a remembrance to Kyle. I'd like to find a nice spot to display it in honor of him, but first I want to be sure Mackenzie is okay with that. Why don't you go ahead and have it moved to my garage for now. My bike is in there also."

"Great and thanks for helping with the house. I do need to get the baby's room painted so if you want to help with that, I'd appreciate it. I was going to call around for a painter later this week."

"I'll take care of it."

"I don't know how long she's planning on being gone though I know she's still planning on returning to work sometime after the baby turns six months old."

"Is she planning to stay in Virginia all of that time?" he asked, hoping not.

"I really don't know. We'll all keep our fingers crossed that she'll return home sooner rather than later."

"I'm with you on that. I don't want the first time I see the baby is when she's already walking and talking."

"Me either, but I'm going down with my parents when she has the baby. Maybe you can come along with

57

us."

"I don't think Mackenzie would want me there, but I'll let you know."

"For now, I'm going to do what I can to keep this place up so that it's one less thing for her to worry about."

"I agree and anything you need me to do to help, all you have to do is ask and I'm there."

"Thanks Trey. Take this key and I'll get my mom's copy. You'll need it to get in and out if you need to while you're keeping the grass cut and everything. Now that you're back pretty much for good, what's next for you besides the business? Are you looking forward to breaking many hearts?"

He smiled as again, his reputation proceeded him and Kyle apparently told too many of his stories to Carmen.

"What?" he asked innocently while shrugging his shoulders.

"Don't play coy with me lover boy. You know that irresistible charm you have that makes women take a third and fourth look at you when you walk by."

As soon as Carmen said the words, a woman walking by looked up at them and eyed Trey from head to toe. She knew that kind of behavior happened everywhere he went. She watched as the woman nearly tripped because she couldn't take her eyes off of him. The look on the woman's face and in her eyes said that she was picturing him naked and would like to have a front row seat the next time he was. When she licked her lips before looking away, Carmen slapped him on the arm. He was eating up all of that attention.

"See what I'm talking about? She would rather fall and injure herself before she would take her eyes off of you for one second. She didn't even know or care if we were married or a couple. She put it out there that she wanted you. I can tell this is a common thing for you."

Trey laughed.

"I am not interested in that woman, though she is fine."

"All I can say is look out Monterey because Trey Blackwell is back in town and your woman that you thought was yours may not be now that's he's back."

"Oh, you got jokes I see."

"Now you know I've known you practically my whole life and I know of the shenanigans you and my brother had going on with the ladies. Sneaking them in my parents' house when you thought no one was paying attention. You've always had a reputation with the ladies."

"What are you trying to say that I'm using them or something?"

"Trey, don't try to sound all hurt. I'm not saying that and you know it. I've never heard about a woman who has ever said anything bad about you other than you won't commit, but as far as treatment, nothing but kudos my brother," she said slyly.

"I'm not really the commitment type."

"Not even now that you'll soon be back home for good?"

"I was seeing someone recently, but she has a career as a model and jets around the country more than me which doesn't make for a good relationship."

"Oh, Kyle didn't tell me about that."

"As he should not have. I hadn't had a chance to tell him much about her other than that we'd hooked up a few times. He wanted to know more and I told him we would catch up when we both go out."

Trey tone turned somber, something he didn't want to do.

Carmen caught the change in his demeanor.

"No feeling sad right now. He would be happy to know that you were at least open to something more than a one-night stand."

"Well, we'll see. Right now I have a company to get up and running and that's my priority. We'll leave my love life or lack of one to me. I hear you have something pretty serious going on."

"Yeah, it's getting pretty serious. We've been going out for about eight months now and my parents like him, so that's a good start."

"Yeah, well he'll have to pass my test since Kyle isn't here to give him the once over."

"Oh, now we've moved from your love life to mine? I think that's my cue to get back to what I was doing when you drove up."

Trey laughed knowing she was now avoiding his meddling in her personal life, but his was fair game.

"That's how you want to play this? It's okay for you to dive into mine, but I can't get all in yours?"

"That's what I'm saying and when you finally do get a love life, I'll still be all in it. I have to approve of any woman who thinks she can steal your heart. That's a feat I'm not sure any woman will be able to do."

"You may be right about that, but I'll think about keeping you posted."

"Yeah, yeah. Until then, try sneaking women in your back door so that you're not the talk of the town."

Trey laughed so hard his body shook.

"On that note, I'm going to go stop in on your parents real quick to let them know I'm home for good and to see if there is anything they need."

"I think my dad went to play golf with some friends who felt that he needed to get out of the house, but my mom should be there."

Trey waved as he jumped in his truck. It felt good to laugh again and he looked forward to getting some level of normalcy back to his life.

On the drive to Kyle's parents' house, his thoughts turned to concern for Mackenzie. He hoped she and the baby were doing okay. He would give her a few days to settle in and then he'd try reaching out again. He knew dropping in on her in Virginia wouldn't be a good idea and so he'd wait until she returned and hopefully they would be able to talk, heal together and find the peace that they both needed in order to heal. He never skirted on a responsibility before in his life and he wasn't going to start with looking after the family Kyle left behind. He knew what it felt like to have a father gone from his life and he wanted to be sure Mackenzie and Kylie knew that he was there for whatever they needed.

Kyle helped him get through life when his father was no longer around and he planned to be there for his family now that he was gone. It may take Mackenzie a long time, but he now had nothing but time on his hands and he was a patient man.

7

Mackenzie's cell phone chimed again and when she saw the familiar number, she struggled with whether to finally answer or not. She'd been avoiding Trey for a while now. Seeing him and talking to him was going to be too hard and too painful and she wasn't ready for that yet. She'd listened to his many voicemail messages and read all of his texts and though she knew that he meant well, she couldn't handle talking to him yet. She let the call roll over to voicemail.

"You really need to talk to him."

Mackenzie looked up as her father joined her in the sitting room of their home. She was enjoying being back in Virginia with them as she got closer to her due date which was now a few short weeks away.

"I can't right now dad."

"It's been three months Kenzie and it's not his fault."

"I know it's not his fault, but I don't know what to

say. The longer I have waited, the harder it is to talk to him. I have no explanation for ignoring him for three months."

"It's not right to ignore him and have him worrying about you. I know he can check with Kyle's parents to see how you're doing, but he shouldn't have to do that. He and Kyle were the best of friends and he's trying to do what any friend would do and if the roles were reversed, I know that Kyle would do the same thing. Don't shut him out, especially now. He's still hurting as much as you are and maybe it will cheer you up to talk to him. You can't run from that forever especially since you told me he was going to be back in Monterey for good once his tour was finally up. You will see him again and again and I think now is the time to start the healing."

"I know, you're right dad."

Mackenzie looked down at her stomach as imprints of her baby girl's hand appeared on her stomach. Little Kylie sure was a busy little baby. She placed her hand over the little palm print that pushed on her skin and tears began streaming down her face knowing that her little girl will never be able to meet her father.

"We're all here for you and Trey would be too if you let him. I almost forgot what I came in here for. There was a big package delivered for you from your friend Ava. The note with it said it's a present for the baby so I'll put it in your room. Pick up the phone and call Trey back. If he had a wife who was going through what you're going through, do you think you'd avoid her for months? No, you would reach out to comfort her. Stop treating that young man like he doesn't matter."

Mackenzie waited until he left and dialed Trey back. He answered on the first ring.

"Hi Trey," she said softly.

"Hi. How are you and how is the baby?"

"We're both doing well. She has about two more weeks and then it's due day. How are you?"

"I'm doing good, hanging in there. I'm glad you finally called me back," he said softly.

"I'm sorry I haven't called you back and thanks for being concerned about me, but I'm doing pretty good. Are you home yet or still abroad?"

"No, I'm home. I've been back and forth, but pretty much back here for good now. I have a few more months, but mostly that's just processing with no assignments. I hear you're in Virginia."

"Yes, I needed to breathe and I couldn't do that at home and so I decided to come home with my parents, have the baby here and spend some time relaxing."

"I hope you'll send me some pictures of the baby after you have her. I know she is going to be a beauty."

For the first time in a while, Mackenzie smiled hearing the jubilance in Trey's voice.

"I'll send you tons and I'm warning you to not complain when I send more than you can look at."

"Send as many as you like and a video or two. How long do you plan on staying in Virginia?"

"I hadn't really thought about it, but probably for about six more months. I don't want to fly with the baby being too young and I'm looking for help with her from my mom. If it were up to them I would never go back to California, but I'm going back. My life is there, my job is there and even without Kyle, I still want to live and raise Kylie there."

"I've been helping Carmen care for the house until you get back, cutting the grass and stuff like that. If there is anything in particular you want me to do before you get back, let me know. I'm here to help in any way I can."

"I know you are and thank you for that and I'm sorry for not returning your calls. It wasn't you I was avoiding, but I was angry at you for delivering the news when I know that I wouldn't have wanted it from anyone other than you because it wouldn't have been delivered the same way. I just needed a little time to process everything and figure out what I was going to do next. Silencing everyone around me except for family was what I needed, but I'm glad to be talking to you right now. How are the plans for the business coming along?"

"They are coming along great. We have the property secured and the preliminary work that started a few months back is completed and now we just have to finish making improvements."

"I can't wait to hear about all of the spy stuff you will be doing."

Trey laughed.

"What spy stuff?"

"Don't play with me Trey. Kyle told me that one of

the things you guys would be handling would be some top secret missions that the United States couldn't get involved in without causing the next world war. I bet some of this stuff will be better than any spy novel I could read."

"Yeah, well, I don't know what he told you, but we'll be focused on background checks, providing security and doing some investigations on a small scale," he lied.

"Yeah, right. That's why your partners are ex-Navy SEALs, former SWAT team members, sharp shooters and I won't even speak about Ivan and his knack for disappearing and going unnoticed in a room full of people who know him. Don't worry, your secrets are safe with me, but every now and then, tell me a story or two. I love this stuff!" she proclaimed, happy to be able to smile and laugh again.

"Okay, but on the condition that you stay in touch with me and let me know if you and the baby need anything. I hope you don't stay in Virginia too long because I'd like to see that little one before she's a grown woman."

"Ha, ha, you got jokes, but I hear you. I'm thinking we'll be back in about six months, but with all of this technology and with equipment that your company has that I'm sure would allow you to spy on me without me knowing about it, I promise to stay in contact and face-time so that you can see the baby up close and personal as if she were right there with you."

"I'm going to love that."

"How are things with you now that you are settling into a life post-military? Is it weird?"

"Not really because this had been the plan for so long that I was already getting accustomed to thinking about life that didn't involve a different country, sometimes several times a week. I'm looking for life to settle down at least for a while. We've already been getting inquiries about the business from companies around the world and we haven't even finished the construction yet. Most of those are from those connected to military higher ups so the faster we can get things up and running, the quicker we can start working some cases. We'll all need to stay busy, at least for a while since that's what we're used to doing."

"What about a personal life? Aren't you ready for that now that you'll be settled into your life as a civilian?"

He laughed out loud.

"What is it with everyone around me trying to push me into love and marriage?"

Mackenzie laughed too.

"Who is everyone?"

"Carmen asked sort of the same type of question a few months ago right after you left. I'm not destitute when it comes to women."

"Trey, you have never been with a woman for more than a night in a town and I know you don't want that forever. Don't you want love, marriage and babies of your own one day?"

"I will have all of that one day when it's my time and

apparently that time isn't now."

"I know you're concerned about me and making sure that I'm moving on with my life in a healthy manner and I want the same for you."

"I can tell you that I'm doing better as more time passes by and now that I've heard from you directly, I won't worry as much as I have been."

"Again, I'm sorry to make you worry like that. There's been so much to process."

"I understand, but I hope that you won't cut me out. I'm here for anything you need."

"Thank you Trey."

"Okay, well I'm going to let you go and hopefully get some rest and make sure someone calls or texts me when you have the baby. I'll check on you early next week or feel free to call me anytime. I'm here for you Mackenzie and I want you to lean on me for whatever you need. You and that baby are family to me and I take care of family."

"I appreciate it Trey and tell everyone I said hello."

When she hung up, she sat staring at the phone mad with herself for waiting so long before reaching out to him. She knew he meant well and she should expect that he'd worry about her. She knew that he would help her get through and she'd do the same for him.

8

Mackenzie couldn't sleep and she knew if she didn't sleep now, there would be no sleep for her once three month old Kylie was woke. She tried every trick in the book, but nothing worked. She took a long, hot bath while her mother kept an eye on Kylie. She tried reading and that didn't work. She even tried counting sheep yet still, she was wide awake as if it were the middle of the day. She thought about calling Ava, but from their conversation earlier, she knew that Ava had to be at the hospital at an ungodly hour and since it was already after eleven at night, she didn't want to disturb her. Carmen was out of the question because she was out on a date with her boyfriend. They'd talked earlier and she had been happy to hear that the relationship was growing. She dared not interrupt her night of romance. Of her other friends, she didn't really have anyone she wanted to talk to and then a vision of Trey entered her mind.

He had been a rock for her through everything. He called or sent a text every day just to check on her and the baby. She assumed it was because she'd recently had a meltdown while talking to him and he was concerned and scared for her. She hadn't meant to scare him, but that sudden feeling of depression came from nowhere, just when she thought she was doing better.

Her first few months in Virginia had been extremely tough. She couldn't get through a second of her day without thinking about Kyle and how she'd never see him again.

She and Trey had been talking about some of their good times and his death once again hit her hard and she cried uncontrollably. She knew she had frightened him because he told her he was minutes away from catching a flight to get to her. It wasn't until she finally calmed down and assured him that she was okay and that she needed to get that out. He promised to always be a sounding board for her and tonight she needed that.

She hated disturbing him thinking he may be at his office or away finishing up his tour. He may even be out on a date and if that was the case, she really didn't want to disturb him. He was entitled to a life not spent catering to her and worrying about her all the time. A few times a week he called her to check in on her or she'd call him to give him an update on how she and Kylie were doing. That had been going on since the day she finally decided to return his many calls to her. They had settled into a routine and she enjoyed every one of their chats. She was learning a lot about him that she didn't know and was happy to see a softer side of him and not just the rough, military exterior persona that she'd grown accustomed to seeing through the years. He was definitely more relaxed now that he was home and she liked this side of him.

Trey had turned into that person that she could share anything with and he wouldn't judge her. When she told him that there were times that she was so depressed that she'd close herself up in a room for a full day. Luckily her mother understood and looked after Kylie, but she couldn't help needing that space. Trey let her know that he understood as she continued to work through her grief. He never told her to get it together or that she was going overboard with her emotions. He supported her and oftentimes talked her head off until she forgot that she was down. By the end of the conversation, he'd have her laughing at his antics.

He would share with her stories of his attempts at dating when his heart wasn't really into it. He even told her stories of women who had no qualms with telling him exactly what they wanted from him. Luckily he'd made the decision that he wanted more than just a different bed partner all the time, but he hadn't found a woman that he wanted more from than that.

Mackenzie knew any woman would be lucky to have a great guy like Trey. He was the type that worshipped a woman and treated her like a queen, something every woman wants from her man. There is nothing he wouldn't do for those he cared about and she should know because he had been there for her from the start just as he said he would be. She didn't want to overstay her welcome of leaning on him all the time even though he told her there was no such thing. Tonight she could really use a good friend.

"I've worried him enough," she said to herself out loud.

Still, she knew that talking to him would release her mind and perhaps she could get to sleep. She reached for her cell phone on the nightstand and before she second guessed herself again, she dialed his number. His phone rang twice before she realized she shouldn't have called so late and was just about to hang up when he answered.

"Kenzie, are you alright?"

Mackenzie knew the late hour call would give him cause for concern.

"Yes, I'm fine and nothing's wrong. I'm sorry for calling you so late and I'm sure I'm disturbing something you were doing."

She felt the need to apologize because once again, she was leaning on him when he probably had his own things to tend to.

"You're not disturbing me. I'm actually just getting in the house."

"You're back in Monterey already? When we talked earlier this week you were out of the country."

"I just got back today."

"Are you sure I'm not bothering you?"

"Mackenzie stop it. You can call me anytime for any reason, you know that. What's up?"

She hated dropping all of her misery on him. He was being such a good friend and every time they talked, she released the weight of the world on him.

"Nothing major. I was having a hard time getting to sleep and I don't know, I thought I would call and hear a friendly voice. My parents and Kylie are all sleeping peacefully, yet I'm up as if it's the middle of the day."

"Well, I'm glad you consider me that friendly voice when you need it. How is Kylie doing?"

"Growing like a weed. I think every time I look at her, there is something new I didn't notice just the moment before."

"I got those last picture you sent me and you're right, she is really growing. I hope to see her before she graduates college," he quipped and then laughed out loud when he heard her laugh too.

"Why does everyone think I'm not going to return home? I promise you Kylie and I will be home. We are definitely coming home for my in-laws anniversary party in a few months. When we do, I'll be back for good. It will be time to get back to my life, the one I've been trying to run away from."

"I wouldn't say you were running away. I know I understand your need for breathing room from the constant memory of being in the house, a house that has been maintained beautifully in you absence," he added.

"Enough about me for a change. We always talk about me and Kylie. Let's talk about you. How is the business coming along?"

"It's finally starting to sink in that we'll be up and running in a few months. I've secured all the licenses we'll need and deliveries are coming in daily with office equipment and in a few months we'll start hiring a few office staff."

"I know you won't be hiring just anybody."

"Of course not. It will have to be someone with a high security clearance level."

"Yet you told me nothing real high level will be handled through you," she replied sarcastically.

"Hey, what you don't know you can't be a witness to, right?" he added comically.

"Funny Trey. What about dating?"

"Nope, still not really dating."

"I'm assuming by not really you mean you're still the old playboy Trey?"

"Not hardly. I seem to have less time now for that than I did before which is surprising, but I think now I'm looking for the right one, not just a right-now one."

"Ah, now that's a different Trey."

"Yeah, well we all have to grow up some time and I guess my time is now. The quality is more important to me than the quantity which is definitely a switch. Like I told Carmen, as soon as I find that, I will let you know."

"Until then though, it's business as usual? Don't cause and riots or outright fighting over you. Carmen told me she saw you out at a club not too long ago and two women were arguing over which one of them would get to go home with you at the end of the night," she laughed.

"Yeah and neither one did since I wasn't interested. Women are something else," he chuckled.

"Oh, so there were other women you took home that night?" she asked, not sure why she was so interested in his personal life. Did she feel a hint of jealousy? She pushed that thought to the side.

"There are no women Kenzie," Trey replied, pointedly.

"Come on, Trey. You can be honest with me. You know Kyle couldn't hold water let alone stories about you and how everywhere you went, women of all ages found you irresistible."

"I don't know about all that, but hey, I wasn't married to the great Mackenzie Ellis so I managed the cards I was dealt. I'm not the first man to enjoy women the way I did."

Trey shocked himself saying did instead of does, which means in the past.

"Do you think there is a perfect woman out there for you?"

"I'm not sure there is a perfect woman for me. I've never taken the time to get to know a woman in order to one day consider her perfect for me or at least enough to fall in love with."

Mackenzie laid back in bed, feeling more comfortable and relaxed than she had all day and she contributed that to the Trey's calm tone. Each time they talked, she realized there was something about his voice that made her want to let go of everything that weighed her down.

"Sure there is Trey. You have to be open to it and willing to give someone a chance. You've spent a lot of years just bedding women and keeping your heart locked away to be sure you weren't vulnerable. You don't have to admit it because I know it when I see it. Whether you want them to or not, women are drawn to you like a moth to a flame."

"Yeah, that's what I'm told, but I don't pay much attention to that and you know any wild stories about me you may have heard are all false," he laughed.

"You're going to be an incredible catch for the right woman one day and I can't wait to see that happen. I have a few friends I can set you up with that I think would be good for you."

"Kenzie, don't even go there. If I was looking for a date, I don't need to be hooked up. Besides, you and your friends share too much and your mind has already been poisoned by who you think I am. No more brainwashing you about me."

"Okay, fair enough, but the offer will forever stand. I think you should have the right woman who will treat you right and give you lots of beautiful babies."

"I don't know about all of that, but I will make you a promise if you make one for me."

"Okay, what's that," she replied.

"If I find the perfect woman and fall in love, you will be the first person I tell and in return you have to promise me that you won't ever think that any phone call or text from you to me is ever a bother or interruption. I'm here for you whenever you need me and if you ever need someone to talk to, you can always talk to me about anything. Deal?"

Mackenzie smiled and yawned.

"Oh, I heard that. Sounds to me like someone is finally sleepy."

"I think I am and thank you for being a good friend. I can't tell you how much it means to me to know that you're here for Kylie and me."

"You and Kylie mean everything to me even if you're on the other side of the country and like I said, I'm here and do we have a deal?" he asked.

"We have a deal."

"Great. Get some sleep and I'll check in on you and Kylie tomorrow. Call me when she's awake so that I can hear her babble in the phone."

"Okay, well goodnight and as usual, thank you. Your friendship helps me to stay strong."

After the call ended, Trey sat down in his favorite chair in his favorite room of his house that he'd labeled his man cave. He was glad Mackenzie had called him when she needed someone to talk to. Her friendship meant more to him than he would admit to anyone and if he were honest with himself, he would admit that for the past month or so, he hasn't been able to think of anything, but her.

Mackenzie's voice rang out in his head at the most inopportune times. She was stunningly beautiful and he could see why Kyle fell head over heels in love with her. She was the quintessence of the perfect woman.

He felt uneasy with his thoughts and tried to shake them off by standing up and pacing back and forth. Unable to shake thoughts he knew he shouldn't be having, he reached for the remote to the television that covered the entire wall and the surround sound came on booming throughout the room.

"What the hell am I thinking?" he said. "I'm going to burn in hell for my thoughts. This cannot be happening. This can't be," he said before sitting back down to try and take his mind off of Mackenzie because he already knew, his thoughts were treading on dangerous ground.

9

Kylie had been fussy all day and Mackenzie knew it was probably due to the two front teeth that were finally cutting through. At seven months old, those two little teeth were wreaking havoc on her ability to get any real sleep at night.

Mackenzie was happy to be back at her home in California and looked forward to going back to work soon. She'd been gone from work for a year and it was time to get back to it.

She looked around her home and thanks to the work of Carmen and Trey, she came back and didn't have much to do other than unpack. She was happy to get back in time to join in the fortieth wedding anniversary party of Kyle's parents. She hadn't seen them since Kylie was three months old which was the last time they had flown to Virginia for a visit.

Kylie and her teething may keep her from attending

the party because she didn't want her crying throughout the evening and she'd have to leave early anyway. She was running out of things to try and Kylie hated them all. She'd given her every object to put in her mouth to sooth her aching gums, but nothing was working. She picked up the phone to let her sister-in-law know that she and Kylie would be staying home.

"Carmen, how are the celebration plans coming along?"

"Are you back?"

"Yes, Kylie and I flew in last night and we're getting settled back in at home. Thanks for keeping the place up while I was away. I wasn't expecting to be gone for a year and if it wasn't due to the anniversary party, I probably would have stayed a little longer. The anniversary of Kyle's death came around and I didn't want to be in California for that."

"I understand. We spend that day quietly here."

"Maybe we can do something soon with all of us."

"I think that would be great."

"Are you getting ready for the party tonight?"

"That's what I was calling about. I didn't sleep at all last night, partly because Kylie had a hard time settling down now that she's teething and because of teething, I'm not sure we'll make it to the party. I won't tell you how terrible the plane ride was with her crying the whole time, but people really sympathized when I explained her teeth were coming in. I don't want her to ruin tonight's festivities with crying since I can't seem to soothe her at all."

"Aw, everyone was looking forward to seeing you both tonight. The party is for them, but believe me, you and Kylie were going to be the highlight of the night. Do you think you can come for a little while? I'm sure we can help look after her and mom and dad already bought a crib and Trey put it up in Kyle's old bedroom at the house. When I told them you were coming home for the party, they went on a shopping spree. They were already planning to take over your baby so be warned."

Mackenzie laughed and smiled because she already knew about the crib and the nursery at their house that was set up. She hated that the family had been waiting for months to see Kylie and she'd have to stay home because of her teething.

"How about if Kylie and I come for a little while and when she starts getting restless, I'll make my exit and get her back home?"

"I think that's a great idea."

"Are you sure you don't need me to do anything for tonight?"

"No, just bring the world's cutest little niece with you and that will be enough for us all."

"Alright, I'm going to try to get her down for a nap and we'll see you at the house tonight."

"Hey, have you told Trey you're back yet? He was here at the house earlier this week finishing up the work on the deck and asked if you'd changed your mind about coming back home."

"I haven't talked to him yet, but I'll see him tonight at the party if he's there."

"He'll be here. Glad to have you back home Kenzie. We really missed you; I really missed you and as soon as you are up to it, we need to get some shopping in."

"Now that I can do anytime. Kylie is growing so fast out of everything and the weather is different here than in Virginia so I need to pick up lots of new things for her."

"Good, we can talk about it later tonight."

After hanging up with Carmen, Mackenzie thought about calling Trey to let him know she was back. The last time they talked, she told him she would be back before the party, but hadn't given him a date. When she didn't, he probably assumed she changed her mind. She was looking forward to seeing him. They were friends, which was true, but something else was brewing. She could feel it every time they talked and there were times when she was disappointed when he didn't call at a time when she thought he would. She longed to hear his voice and smiled when she'd see a text letting her know that he was thinking about her and Kylie. She knew what she was beginning to feel was more than just friendship and it scared her. These were feelings she shouldn't have for someone so close to her.

**

"Trey, why are you still here? Don't you have a party to get to?" Dustin asked.

Trey checked his watch and he was already running behind so being on time for the anniversary party wasn't going to happen.

"Yeah, I do and I'm already late so a little extra

lateness won't really matter. I was looking over the plans for the final phase of the construction and I like what I see. I made a few changes I want you to look at and if they're good with you, pass them on to the crew so that they can start."

"I've got this covered so you can go ahead and make your exit here and your appearance at the party. Before you lie and tell me I don't know what I'm talking about, I'm also going to say stop trying to avoid the inevitable."

Trey looked at him confused.

"I have no idea what's inevitable. What am I avoiding?"

"Mackenzie."

Trey shuffled the papers around on his desk avoiding eye contact with Dustin.

"Don't go there Dustin because there's nothing there."

"Is that why all of a sudden you've turned jumpy? You're aren't often late for anything, yet you're comfortably making yourself late for the party. As long as you've been waiting for Mackenzie to get back here so that you could see for yourself that she's doing okay, you're in no rush to get there."

"I don't even know that she'll be at the party."

"Didn't you tell me that you spoke to Carmen and she told you she was back in town?"

"Yeah, I did, but that doesn't mean she'll be at the party."

"Stop stalling Trey. I think I know the reason and

like I said, it's inevitable so you may as well get it over with and I will be the first to say, don't sweat it. I don't know when it happened, but it did and I'm not saying run out and declare anything to the world. All I'm saying is, don't sit here as if another time to come face to face with her isn't going to come up."

"Dustin, you are way off here."

"Is that what you think? Okay, then let me be frank instead of using my knack for subtlety since you're trying to act like I don't know you or that we haven't been friends for years. You've developed feelings for Mackenzie Ellis and you're trying your best to hide it because of who she is. I've known you a lot of years and I know how you are when it comes to women. For you they are fun to play with and move on, but you've never found any kind of connection with any."

Trey stood up harder and faster than he expected.

"Are you insane? She's Kyle's wife and off limits."

"No, she was Kyle's wife. I love and miss him as much as you do, but she's no longer married to him, he's been gone a year and over the past several months when I ask you about her and Kylie, there is a complete change in your posture and personality when it comes to talking about her."

"I'm trying to look after her just as I know Kyle would do if it were me. We all have a responsibility to look after them now that he's no longer with us. I'm just doing what I know he would expect and I wouldn't dishonor him by making a play for her."

"Trey, you don't have to convince me because it's not

working, but feel free to repeat that several times a day if that's what it will take to convince yourself. She's a beautiful woman and it wouldn't take much for any man to find her attractive inside and out. You have grown close to her with all of your late night phone conversations and through the hurt of losing Kyle, I think it's brought the two of you together unexpectedly. You're denying it because deep down you feel it's wrong. I'm telling you it's not wrong as long as what you are feeling is genuine. She's not one of those play things you connect with from one city to another or one country to another; she's special and deserves the best that life has to offer her after the hand that was played to her over a year ago."

Trey moved about his office trying not to pay attention to the truth that came out of Dustin's mouth. He was right, but the last thing that was going to happen was any admission. He didn't know when it happened, but staying in constant contact with Mackenzie for the past seven months surprised him with feelings for her that he wasn't expecting. What kind of friend to Kyle is he for thinking of Mackenzie the way he had been lately? There was no way he could act on what he was feeling, a feeling that rammed into him like a truck. There are plenty of women who would be easily obtainable if he were interested, but Mackenzie should not be on the list of women he's interested in. He needed to shake it off and there was no need to continue lying to his friend. He turned to face Dustin.

"I can't do it; it's not right. I must be out of my mind."

"You're not out of your mind. You can't help the woman you fall for."

"I won't even tell you the number of women I've been with just since I've been back home and not one of them, not one of them even comes close to making me feel anything for them for more than just a bed warmer. When it comes to Mackenzie, I can't stop thinking about her. The only thing I know is that for the past two months at least, she's on my mind constantly and when I heard that she was finally coming home, I haven't been able to think of anything else other than what's going to happen when I finally come face to face with her. I can't fall for her; I can't."

Dustin came round to face his friend who was clearly torn by his admission.

"I think saying you can't is no longer on the table. What is on the table is, what are you going to do about it? I know it seems sudden and strange, but you can't help that there is something there. There is no way to tell if it's mutual in any sense of the word unless you actually see and talk to her face to face. I won't say hit her with any of the feelings you have, but don't avoid her because that would be worse than anything. It seems that she has come to count on you as a friend as much as you've come to count on her friendship, so don't back away from it. Maybe nothing will come out of it and once you see her, you'll see that nothing is there and it was just something that played in your head because you've grown close through conversation. Either way, get your ass to that party, celebrate his parents and Mackenzie's return and try to have a good time."

"I don't know. I think I'm setting myself up for something I'm not ready to face head on yet."

"You're ready and however you decided to go about this, you have my one hundred percent support. I don't want to you see you hide from the fact that you want more than just friendship from Mackenzie. If it were me, I wouldn't fight it, but confront it and figure out a way to handle it with her very carefully. It may come down that your friendship means more to her than moving beyond that and I know you'll respect that."

"Damn right I will. I wouldn't want to do anything to hurt her including falling for her if it means we would no longer be friends. I'm going to leave the plans here for you to look over and I'll check with you tomorrow about it when I get here to the office. Thanks for the advice and always kicking me into gear."

"Hey, I'm here to kick anyone who needs it," Dustin joked.

10

The party was in full swing and thankfully, so far Kylie hadn't been disruptive though she wouldn't let anyone touch her other than Mackenzie. People had been coming up to her all night to meet Kylie and Kylie was her usual self, not interested in anyone touching her and definitely not taking her from her mother's arms, not even her in-laws. Mackenzie made apologies explaining that Kylie was teething and everyone understood.

After about an hour, she was able to lay Kylie down in the crib her in-laws put up for her and then spend a little time enjoying the party.

"Welcome home."

Mackenzie turned at the sound of Trey's deep, husky voice.

"Trey," she said launching herself into his arms. "You're here!"

"Hey, I wouldn't miss this party for anything. The Ellis' are my second parents. I'm happy to see you back home. We've all missed you and of course I can't wait to see that little lady of yours."

"I put her down a little while ago. She's been fussy and non-social to everyone at this party including family. I'll be an extremely happy mother when those two teeth that have been keeping us both from getting any sleep finally do come in."

"Well, hopefully she'll wake up before I leave and I'll get a chance to say hello."

"Okay, but don't say I didn't warn you when she gives you the cold shoulder."

"It's good to see you Kenzie and you look beautiful."

"Thank you. You clean up nice," she replied.

Any thoughts that she was in trouble when it came to Trey were confirmed the minute she laid eyes on him. His smile was captivating and he had eyes that were damn near erotic. These were all things that she'd never noticed about him before.

She thought about their many conversations and all that they shared and now standing in front of him, he seemed different to her. He wasn't just Kyle's friend anymore. He was Trey Blackwell, a fine specimen of a man and with his intense stare, she felt things fluttering in her stomach as if she were a nervous teenager.

She known Trey for years, but something was different today. He'd always been tall, most likely around six feet since she was five foot seven and he towered over her by almost six inches. She never noticed how broad his shoulders were or how muscular his arms were, something she could see through the form fitting dress shirt he'd worn. He was talking, but she couldn't hear a word he was saying because her thoughts had carried her to a place far beyond their conversation especially after he leaned back on the counter, crossing his legs at the ankles and putting his attention full on her.

The warm summer night appeared to be getting even hotter. She wanted to fan herself, but she didn't want to look awkward since she appeared to be the only one feeling the heat.

Making an attempt to check back in to the conversation, she looked up into his face and the light brown tone of his skin and neatly trimmed goatee reminded her of Shemar Moore, one of her favorite actors. She knew that people were always teasing him because he looked like the gorgeous actor. Trey could definitely pass as a near twin for him. He had the same type of close haircut and when he smiled, it made her think that all that glittered truly was gold. The man was a masterpiece and her body was reminding her that she was a woman. She shivered realizing who she was thinking about and in what manner she was thinking about him. She had to check to be sure no one saw her ogling him.

"Did you hear me?"

Mackenzie snapped out of it when she realized she was missing the bulk of the conversation with him.

"I'm sorry, what did you say?"

"I was asking if you were settling back in at home and if you were having a good time at the party so far."

Yeah, she was definitely in the twilight zone because she didn't hear any of that. What she did hear was Kylie waking up.

"Sounds like someone is awake," she said when whimpers came across the baby monitor on her hip.

"Do you want me to get her?" Carmen asked.

"I wish, but I don't think she'll let anyone touch her. It's amazing what two teeth can do to a baby with a sweet personality. I'll go get her and we'll probably make our exit after I give her a bottle."

"I'll go with you to get her. I want to see her before you leave. It seems like she's been sleeping the whole time."

"You're going to wish she still was in a few short minutes when she lights this party up with her screams."

"I'll be back," she said to Trey.

When Carmen had already exited the room, Trey leaned closer to her and whispered.

"I'll be right here," he said.

To Mackenzie it sounded like he was crooning, but she knew it had to be her imagination. She had been having weird thoughts about him and it was only fair that he sounded like a romantic interest in his response. She smiled, nodded and left to get her now crying baby.

Kylie wasn't planning on giving anyone any peace so

Mackenzie looked around for her purse and keys to get her home. As she entered the kitchen and this time with Kylie in her arms, true to his word, Trey was still standing in the same spot looking just as good as he had before she exited. She was in trouble, she thought.

"I'm going to get Kylie home before she screams the roof off of the house."

"You mean my first real look at her and you're already taking her home?"

"Hi Kylie," he said playfully hoping to help quiet her crying. He wasn't all that good with children since he hadn't spent a lot of time around them. Kylie was a beauty. At seven months, she had a head full of thick black hair held in place by several pink and white barrettes. She had big, beautiful eyes that were turning red because she was crying so hard.

Mackenzie tried to bounce her and hold up her little hand to say hello to Trey, but she wasn't having it; that made her cry even harder.

"Hey, pretty little lady. What's with all this noise huh?" Trey said, moving away from the counter and coming up close.

Mackenzie watched as a screaming Kylie suddenly quieted the moment she looked up and laid eyes on him. Trey smiled and cooed at her and surprisingly, Kylie smiled back. When he reached out his arms to her, Mackenzie figured Kylie would shy away and clamber up her chest until she could wrap her little arms around her neck, but she didn't. Kylie put her arms out for Trey and he took her into his arms and continued to coo and talk to her. Everyone in the room, which included her in-laws and Carmen were stunned when Kylie quieted completely, laid her head on Trey's shoulder and after a few seconds of him rocking back and forth with her, she was asleep.

"What kind of touch is that? I see that charm doesn't just work on grown women," Carmen jested.

"Yeah, yeah, whatever. Women of all ages love me, especially the young who haven't learned to stay away from me yet," he chuckled.

"I can't believe she went to you so easily. She never goes to anyone, especially anyone she's never met," Mackenzie said.

"That's amazing," Carmen replied. "She wouldn't come to me or my parents when she got here. Maybe it's because she's had a nap."

"What can I say, I have an appeal that can work magic even on the most stubborn," Trey responded.

"Well, I'll have to put you on the schedule for daily drop-ins every time she's moody," Mackenzie said smiling.

Trey smiled back and his heart sped up at her beauty. He was in trouble and he knew it. Thankfully no one in the room was a mind reader or he would be in a heap of trouble and finding ways to explain himself.

"Did you still want to leave or do you want me to lay her back down?"

"Go ahead and lay her down. As long as she's asleep, I'll hang around."

Mackenzie watched as Trey exited the kitchen leaving everyone standing around looking puzzled.

"I see Kylie has a new best friend," her mother-in-law said.

"Yeah, I see that," was all Mackenzie could think to say. What she didn't say was that Kylie wasn't his only fan.

Thinking back, she tried to remember when things had changed for her and she started seeing Trey as more than just a friend.

It started about a month ago when she called him one evening when she couldn't sleep and though he lied and said he was awake, he stayed up and talked to her until she was ready to go to sleep. That had happened many, many times and he never turned her away and would stay on the phone until she was ready to get off. They continued to share a lot about each other. They couldn't talk about the same boring things all the time and as time went on, they discovered more and more to talk about.

He was one of the most kindhearted people she'd ever met, something men don't want to always be known for. It's always one of the first things she liked once she got to know someone. What was she going to do with these thoughts she's been having about him? She had to find a way to stop.

"She's down and sleeping peacefully. What do you say I go grab us some cake?" Trey said to everyone in the room.

"I could use some cake," Carmen exclaimed.

Trey exited the room followed by her parents, right before Carmen turned to Mackenzie.

"I swear, if I didn't already have a man."

"What, Trey? You need to stop," Mackenzie laughed.

"Come on Kenzie, I know who he is, but you can't tell me that man is not fine."

"I didn't say that. All I'm saying is that you do have a man so cut it out."

"Do you think you'll ever get involved with someone again after Kyle? I know I've asked before, but now it's a year later."

"I don't know. Don't you think it's too soon to be talking to me about love and relationships with other men?"

"There is never a bad time to fall in love when you're single and I know it's hard to fathom, but sis-in-law, you are a single, vibrant woman. How much time do you think needs to go by before you decide you need love in your life again?"

Mackenzie hadn't thought about that because she'd had no reason to. She had Kylie and was focusing all of her time and attention to her. One day she may venture back out into the dating game, but she didn't think it would be happening anytime soon.

"If I did think about doing that, I think I'd spend too much time comparing any man I would meet to Kyle and he just can't be topped."

"There are plenty of men who are just as great as Kyle. Take Trey for instance and trust me every woman wants him. Most want him from what they see on the outside and it's a lot to look at that man is so fine. You know I've been looking at them bowed-legs since I was a young girl and I swear if I didn't have a man I'd see what all the stories are about."

"Don't you think he's more like family and should be off limits?"

Carmen looked at her and laughed.

"Girl, there is family and then there is family. Trey is like family, but he isn't family. Besides being gorgeous and built like a lascivious god-like hunk, he's caring, giving, kind, handy and the perfect gentleman. That's proof that good men are out there and there is one for you too when you're ready. I'm going to go chase down my cake. Don't leave before letting me know so that I can kiss my niece good night even if I have to do it from a distance because she doesn't like anyone except Trey. See, even she knows," Carmen kidded before leaving.

Mackenzie stood alone thinking about Carmen's parting words. One thing was accurate and that was that men like Kyle do exist and she was right that a true example of that is Trey.

Even though Carmen explained her thoughts on Trey not really being family and therefore not off limits, to her, he was as off limits as they come. She was ashamed that her thoughts were making her think that Trey was beginning to be more to her than just a friend. Perhaps it was because of the lack of male companionship and Trey was the available man in her life so she felt drawn to him. Perhaps Carmen was right and she should consider a date or two if someone asks

her out. It can't be Trey, she admitted to herself. No
way; it can't be him.

11

Mackenzie entered the hospital with an uneasy feeling. This wasn't the plan she'd made for her life, but she knew that plan had changed the moment Kyle had died and it was time for her to get back to some semblance of normalcy for her and Kylie and work was the best thing for her right now. She was looking forward to getting back to her patients.

The halls of the hospital seemed to be extremely quiet as she made her way to her office. Usually she'd be running into one doctor or another since the hallway was full of doctor's personal offices, but today, she saw no one. Perhaps there was a meeting she hadn't been aware of. Either way, she was making it to her office without running into a lot of people knowing that many would still want to offer her condolences after a year.

She reached for the doorknob to her office and before she could push, it swung open and inside were a bunch of hospital staff, doctors, nurses and others. There were smiling faces everywhere with the room filled with balloons and a table was set off to the side covered with food including a cake with the words, 'welcome back' written across it.

"Welcome back Dr. Ellis!" everyone shouted while clapping.

She looked around at everyone, appreciative that they took the time to welcome her back, helping to make her transition back to work a smooth one. She saw Ava, of course, and she knew it was probably Ava who'd decided to put this celebration together. She also saw Carmen, the doctor who had been using her office while she was out and other doctors, some she knew and some she didn't because they were new.

"Wow, thank you everybody. This is a wonderful surprise."

Mackenzie watched as the chief of surgery for the hospital stepped forward along with the hospital administrator.

"We wanted you to know that we missed you and how happy we are that you're back."

"I'm happy to be back," she said and meant it.

"We want you to take your time easing back into your busy schedule and I've already instructed Ava to kick you out of the hospital at the exact time that you're supposed to leave. I don't want you overdoing it."

Mackenzie smiled. One of the reasons she'd selected the hospital for her residency was not only because it was one of the top hospitals in the country, but because the people were great to work with. They really were like a family. She was about to take a bite of the cake that had been handed to her when Ava walked over.

"I'm so happy to see you back in Monterey and back to work. This place hasn't been the same since you left. How are you and Kylie really doing now that you're back?"

"Well, we've been back about two weeks now and so far it's been pretty good. You know you don't have to avoid coming by the house, which I know you've been dying to do. We're doing okay."

"I know. I wanted to give you some time to settle in and I knew that a lot of people have probably been stopping by and I didn't want to be another person to overwhelm you by invading your space."

"It's okay. Carmen has been wonderful and Kelsey stopped by yesterday with enough food cooked and packaged to last me a lifetime of not having to cook anything. All I have to do is pull stuff out of the freezer and heat it up. She also bought by a lot of baby food and snacks for Kylie. Everyone has been so nice. I also got your gift cards and fruit which I love since you know I'm a fruit fanatic. Trey has also been by a few times since the anniversary party. I'm trying to get Kylie's room all done and he's been a good friend."

"Hmm," Ava said and looked away.

Mackenzie caught that strange look on her face.

"What does that mean?"

"What does what mean?"

"Stop it Ava. I'm not in the mood for twenty

questions," she bantered.

"As your friend, I've always been honest with you and I'm not going to change that today," Ava said looking around at who may be within ear shot to hear them. Seeing no one, she continued on.

"The last two months or so before you returned home and we would talk on the phone, Trey's name came up a lot, mainly from you. You were always telling me how nice he was and how much you had counted on him and a few times you asked me if he was seeing anyone that I knew of since he returned home for good. You spoke about him as if he was more than just a friend to you."

Mackenzie looked away, not sure how to respond since she knew Ava was right. Something about her friendship with Trey changed in there many, many days and nights of talking. During the last month, she would watch the clock knowing a quick evening phone call for them to chat was coming up and she couldn't wait to talk to him. She didn't know what was going on, but something had changed and the thought of that scared her. Thinking of him as more than just a friend was not something she should be thinking about.

She and Trey would talk about everything that was going on in their lives and a few times, he shared with her how he'd gone out on a few dates and for the first time, he wasn't just trying to get them in bed for sex. He was dating in hopes of finding more, but for some reason, he felt distracted. He had been attracted to the women and there was nothing wrong with any of them other than the fact that he felt like he was pushing himself to find the right woman to bring some balance into his life.

"That's absurd, Ava and you know it."

"Do I? Do you? Look at me Kenzie."

Mackenzie turned around and faced her.

"What do you want me to say?"

"The truth."

"Okay, Ava, fine. You want the truth? Something happened and I don't know what it is, but I do know it's wrong and I have to stop it."

Mackenzie felt her pulse quicken realizing she had just shared her deepest thoughts with Ava, thoughts that she'd been holding in afraid of telling anyone. What would people think if she shared that her feelings for Trey had turned from mere friendship to something more?

"Come with me," Ava said, pulling her out of the room and into a vacant office across the hall where they could talk.

"I hear how you talk about Trey and I know that whatever is going on is probably not a one way street. I think you both are struggling with some pretty strong feelings."

"Ava, we can't have any kind of feelings for each other. It would be wrong and I mean wrong on the highest level. I'm thinking he and I are both struggling with Kyle's loss and we've gravitated toward each other and no matter what, it can't end well. You have to promise me you won't say anything to anyone."

"I would never, ever do that, but I'm your friend and let me be the first to tell you that it's okay. Trey is a great guy and I know you didn't set out to be attracted to him, but through everything that you both have been through, it's possible it's bringing you together and rather than fight it, why don't you just live in the moment and go with your heart."

"It's wrong Ava!"

"Why because it's Trey? You're single and so is he. I understand who he is, but make it into more than it has to be. It's what you want it to be and if you don't want it to be anything, then that's fine and you can go back to living your life, but if you want to explore anything, don't you dare back down from it because you are worried about what other people will say. This is still your life and you don't have to answer to anyone, but yourself. You know I'm here for you with whatever you decide to do. Whew, I'm glad I got that out. I've been wanting to say something for a few days now and didn't know how to bring the subject up."

"Do you think anyone else has picked up on anything? What about Carmen?"

"If they have, I'm sure they would have said something by now."

Mackenzie had to shake it off and then let it go. She had enough to deal with in life to not add any drama to the equation.

"I can't put Trey in an awkward position and I would be devastated if anything ruined our friendship. Did I tell you how Kylie is all in love with him?"

"What are you talking about?"

"Remember how I told you that one of the struggles with Kylie is that she doesn't like anyone. She's very fussy and particular about who she lets pick her up. Though she will laugh and play from a distance, try to pick her up and she goes ballistic. At the anniversary party, she was teething terribly that day and I gave her what I could, but nothing would calm her down. Trey went to pick her up and I thought she would scream her head off. She shocked us all when she reached her arms out for him, laid her head on his shoulder and quieted down and went back to sleep. The few times that he's been to the house since then, as soon as she sees him, she lights up and sticks her chubby little arms out for him to pick her up. She laughs and smiles and giggles while playing with his face and if anyone tries to take her from him, it sets off a new world war."

They laughed.

"See, even Kylie knows a good man when she encounters one. I'm not trying to push you into anyone's arms because only you know when you're ready and when you are, you'll have my full support and I don't care who it's with as long as he treats you and Kylie like precious gold. Otherwise, I'd have to get one of my girls to help me hide his body," Ava retorted.

"Girl, I don't think there is anything there other than a mutual respect and kinship because of what we both have been through and that's what I'm going to contribute it to and move on. Thanks for having my back and always telling me things the way I need to hear them. Now let's get back to this celebration before someone comes looking for us."

"Yeah, lets and in the meantime, I think you need a girl's night out; something we haven't done since before you were pregnant with Kylie. I'm going to call Kelly, Kelsey and Carmen and we are going out to take you out to this new spot that everyone is talking about that has a live band on one floor and a DJ on the second level. I hear the food is the best around, too. What do you say to going out and letting our hair down?"

"I don't know Ava. I'd need to get a babysitter for Kylie and I just told you she doesn't take to a lot of people."

"No excuses Kenzie. Ask your mother-in-law to watch her for a few hours and I'm sure she'll be fine. I think you need this and I know you need your girls around you. Go for a little while and when you feel you've had enough, leave and make your way home, but at least give it a try."

Mackenzie chewed on her bottom lip giving it some serious thought.

"Okay, I'm in. Give me enough notice so that I can get a babysitter lined up. A night out could be exactly what I need."

"Good. Let's plan for two weeks from now. That band I was talking about will be back in town then. That gives you a couple of weeks to get a babysitter."

Mackenzie wasn't sure what she'd just agreed to, but she hoped by then, she wouldn't chicken out. It had been a long time since she'd been out.

They linked arms as sisters often do and headed back over to the party.

Mackenzie plastered on a smile while inside, she thought about Trey. Now that she'd said out loud to someone what she'd been going through, it made it all the more real to her. She was falling for Trey Blackwell, the one person she knew she should stay clear of.

12

Happy that Kylie went down easily for her afternoon nap, Mackenzie was able to plan for her night out. In a few hours Carmen would be by to pick up Kylie for the weekend. Tonight was the big girl's night out that Ava had planned for her and a few of their friends. Carmen hadn't had a lot of time with Kylie on her own since they'd moved back into the house and so she offered to keep Kylie for the weekend to allow her some time to let her hair down. She was looking forward to some time out with the ladies and she could get a reprieve from another night of thinking about Trey.

Thoughts of him had begun invading the hours when she should be asleep.

Trey had come by a few times since the party and they'd sat and talked. One evening he had planned to stop by quickly to drop off a gift he'd bought for Kylie and ended up staying to play with her and her new toy until exhaustion over took her and she crawled into his lap and fell asleep. Still the connection Kylie felt to him astounded her. The minute she heard his voice, she would crawl faster than some people could walk and holler until he picked her up.

Whatever she was feeling grew with each passing day and the more she tried to push the thoughts out of her head, the more her body reminded her that this was not a passing interest or just the fact that she was lonely for a man's touch. She wanted Trey's touch. She closed her eyes and thought about what it would feel like to have him caress her back or hold her in his big, strong arms.

"Kenzie, are you alright?" Trey asked coming into the room. She forgot he had been there installing child security devices throughout the house since Kylie loved crawling around. His appearance startled her since her mind had been on him and not just in a friendly way.

"I'm fine," she lied.

"You looked lost in thought there for a minute."

"Oh, that was nothing," she said turning away to avoid his stare. She'd started doing that whenever he was around, afraid he'd see more in her eyes than she wanted him to see.

"Are you sure? I still have a few minutes before I have to get out of here. I have plans later, but I'm here if you need to talk about anything."

Mackenzie looked beyond him, trying not to make eye contact.

"How did all of the child-proofing installations go?"

she asked.

"Everything is good. All of the sockets are covered, she can't open any of the cabinets or doors on her level and I've covered all sharp edges. It's a good thing you're doing this because the last time I was here, she was crawling everywhere and exploring. Wait until she starts walking and learns how to climb on things."

"Yeah," was all she said and moved around him when he walked up a little too close for comfort. He wasn't doing anything other than what he always did, but it was her reaction to him that was giving her cause. This was not the time for her to be thinking about him romantically.

"Are you sure nothing's wrong?"

Trey watched her body language and saw that she was being evasive.

"Why do you ask?" she asked nonchalantly as she faked wiping a table that was already spotless.

"You're talking to me and ignoring me at the same time. Am I here at a bad time?"

"No."

Trey looked at her concerned, knowing something was wrong. This was not the Mackenzie he'd been encountering lately. Today, something was wrong and he had a feeling it had something to do with him.

"Mackenzie?"

When she ignored him he called her name again.

"Mackenzie, there isn't even a hint of dust on that table. If you want me to leave, just tell me, but clearly something is going on."

She stopped mid wipe and started to cry.

"Whoa," he said coming up, turning her around and pulling her into his arms. "Whatever is going on, I'm here."

Without thinking she did something she had never done the many times that he'd hugged her; instead of embracing him around his waist while he hugged her tight, she lifted her arms up and encircled his neck, a move that was more intimate than she realized until she'd done it. Now she realized, it was too late to remove them because to begin with, it felt good and second, it felt damn good!

"I'm sorry," she whispered against his chest.

Being this close to him, her mind reeled with thoughts he Trey felt like an incredible specimen of rugged delight.

"What are you sorry for?"

Trey tried to pull back in order to look her in the face and when he did, she pulled him back in.

"I don't know how to explain this."

"You're scaring me," he said.

Mackenzie cried a little more.

"Okay, I'll just stand here for as long as you need me to and I won't say a word."

"I don't want that," she said.

"Then what do you want."

Mackenzie didn't speak. She leaned back without taking her arms from around his neck and looked up at him, knowing that her eyes were going to tell him everything. She already knew that she had the kind of eyes that never lied when it came to expressing how she was feeling.

Trey didn't say anything when Mackenzie looked up at him. He thought he would see hurt for whatever she was going through, but he didn't. He saw affection, want and an insatiable need. He'd been with enough women to know how to read the signs on their faces and in their eyes, but this was Mackenzie. He may have thoughts about her that no one other than Dustin knew about, but acting on them was another story.

He's spent a lot of time fighting back any feelings he'd been developing for her and Mackenzie was feeling it too and if he was correct, she was frightened about what it meant.

He was afraid to speak knowing he would probably say the wrong thing. Instead he reached to wipe away the tears that were covering her cheeks.

"You know you're not in this alone," he uttered softly.

"I don't think you understand," she responded.

"I believe you think I don't understand, but I do."

"Trey, I don't think we're talking about the same thing."

To prove his point, he caressed her cheek, never taking his eyes from hers. He needed her to see and feel that he understood clearly.

Mackenzie's words got lost in the hitch in her voice, keeping her from speaking. What she saw looking back at her were eyes that she knew matched hers. His were blazing with a carnality she'd never seen staring back at her before. Trey had fallen into the same pit of despair that she was in; fighting a desire that to others might seem indecent. Not only had she developed feelings for him, but it was clear to her that he had feelings for her too. Apparently he did understand.

They stood like that for what seemed an eternity with neither moving nor saying anything. The only sounds heard were of the clock ticking on the wall and their amatory, breathless intakes of breath. Mackenzie felt a heat rise as she watched Trey's eyes dart from her eyes and then down to her lips. A need within her that she'd never experienced before resonated through every part of her body arousing a desperate need stemming from her most intimate parts. She wanted to scream out to the world how just looking at him gave her a wantonly feeling of longing. Every time he looked down at her lips, she felt the need to lick across them to moisten them for him.

Strength she didn't know she had allowed her to follow suit and she looked from his eyes to his lips, letting her eyes rest there for a minute before going back to his eyes.

"You're killing me," he whispered so low, she barely heard him.

Mackenzie didn't know what to say. She didn't know whether to move out of his embrace, raise up on her toes to meet him halfway or run for the hills. All she knew was that in this moment in time, nothing existed except for her and him.

"Mackenzie," he said again and this time he leaned a

little closer to her.

Trey knew he was crossing a line and in fact, he had the moment he looked down at her lips. They appeared to be calling out for him and he wanted to answer in the worse way by ravishing her. He felt like she had cast a spell that captivated and dazzled him like no other woman had before. Now that he knew that he wasn't in this struggle alone, the temptation grew and was now out of his control. He needed to save them both so he pulled her back close to his chest so that he couldn't see her waiting lips. He needed to reign control of his body and his senses before he did something like actually kiss her.

Once he pulled her in close he was a goner the moment he felt her arms tighten a little more around his neck.

"What are we doing Kenzie?" he uttered.

"I don't know," he heard her reply softly as he felt her heart beating profusely in her chest as it rapidly sped to match her increasing breathing pattern.

He no longer wanted to think or even doubt himself. He wanted to feel and he wanted to feel her.

Without giving any more thought and throwing caution to the wind, Trey pulled back slightly and before his next breath, he leaned down and placed a soft kiss on her lips. He shifted his mouth and placed another soft kiss at the corner of her lips and when she sighed in anticipation and desire he captured her lips with a vivacity that only a starving man could understand, kissing her slowly until she actively returned the kiss. He couldn't help himself as he deepened the kiss and they dueled indulging in the hedonistic feelings being shared between them. It was clear that this had been building up for them both for a while.

Trey wasn't sure know how long it had been since she'd found something more than friendship was developing between them, but for him it seemed like a lifetime of wanting her, needing her and the feeling was beyond anything he'd expected. In truth, it wasn't a life time; it had only been a few months. Gone was doubt and reservation about the decision to kiss her and what replaced it was pure satisfaction to the point that he felt hypnotized and would gladly do anything she asked.

Mackenzie was floating on a cloud of hunger and yearning and she never wanted to come down. Trey's lips were embracing every part of her and not just her lips. She felt his kiss in parts of her body that had not been stirred in a long time. She was so caught up in it that she barely heard the moaning surrounding her in the room. Reality set in when she realized the moan was coming from her and then sense settled back into her brain as she broke off the kiss and stood back from him.

Trey saw the look of fear on her face as she took in what they'd just done.

"Umm, whatever this is, I think we both need to take a step back and clear our heads."

"I'm sorry Mackenzie."

"Don't apologize because it wasn't just you, it was

me too, but now we need to stop."

"This was all me and I'm sorry."

"Stop apologizing. That kiss was not your fault."

"Yes it was Kenzie and I should have known better," he said wiping his lips with the back of his hand. He was so engrossed in it that her essence still lingered there.

She moved to the other side of the room, gathered her composure and turned back to face him."

"We should know better. Maybe you should leave and I should go get ready before Carmen gets here to pick up Kiley for the weekend."

This was bad, he thought; very bad.

"I think we need to talk Kenzie."

"No we don't," she retorted quickly. "At least not at this moment. I can't talk about his right now."

"Don't get in the dumps about this. Neither of us planned this and it just sort of happened."

She looked at him confused.

"You and I both know that didn't just happen. I saw in your eyes what I'm sure you saw in mine and what happened has been building up, but that doesn't mean right now is the time to talk about it."

He relented.

"Okay, I'm going to leave, but I feel the need to apologize again if I've made you uncomfortable or if this has crossed a line we can't come back from. I won't lie and say I haven't thought about this, but I will say I should have stopped it."

"I think there is enough blame to go around here. I

kissed you back so there is no need for an apology, but what I do think we need is some space to gather our heads."

"I'm going to leave, but promise me if you want to talk about this that you'll call me."

She looked over at him and as much as she wanted to actually comfort him knowing how bad he felt about the line they'd crossed, she was afraid any more contact would lead them back to what got them here, so she kept her distance.

"I promise."

Trey didn't say anything else before turning to leave. He stopped at the door before going out, but didn't turn around.

"I'm not sorry for the kiss. I know this is dangerous ground, but we gave into something and it's not going to go away because I'm leaving. "

He didn't wait for her to respond before finally leaving.

13

Trey walked inside of his house and slammed the door so hard behind him it rattled. Never had he been more disappointed in himself than he was at the moment. For months, he'd been having thoughts and dreams about Mackenzie, but never in his right mind did he ever plan to follow through on anything. He'd kissed her and though the feeling was incredible, he knew he shouldn't have up until the moment that their lips had touched. She'd felt incredible in his arms and the way she looked at him wanting him as much as he wanted her, he needed to ease the ache he knew they both were experiencing.

After leaving her house, he'd driven around with no destination in mind. All thoughts of hanging out with the fellas was the furthest thing from his mind. He was too busy ripping into himself for making such a move on Mackenzie of all people. He led by his heart and not by his head and though he knew they were on the same page, it was still wrong. He didn't struggle as much with himself when it was just a thought in his head, but the minute he acted on it, he should have known things would be ruined. It had taken her months to even call him in the beginning. Why would he be stupid enough to take such a risk?

Even now, though she'd practically thrown him out of her house, he wanted her like he'd never wanted another woman before in his life. What he couldn't understand was what kind of cosmic intervention was going on that led him to this point? Everything about wanting Mackenzie was wrong despite the feelings. He wasn't just lusting for her because the moment his lips touched hers, he was in love with her. He fought the feeling that he was before that moment, but that was when he knew for sure.

Mackenzie's response to him was more than he could have ever imagined. Her lips were soft and pliant under his assault and her tongue tasted sweet as he savored the tender taste of her.

'You're going to hell for this,' he told himself, just before his cell rang and of course his timing couldn't be more perfect.

"What?" he answered.

"Whoa tiger. What's going on with you?"

"Guess."

Trey knew he couldn't lie; not to Dustin.

119

"Mackenzie. What did you say to her?"

"It wasn't so much what I said, but what I did."

"Do I really want to know?"

He didn't immediately answer not sure he wanted to tell anyone, not even Dustin.

"If you're calling about tonight, I'm not in the mood so I'm going to stay in. We can celebrate the business another time."

"Come on, man. It cannot be that bad. What did you do?"

"I kissed her."

There was a pause and Trey thought maybe Dustin hadn't heard him.

"That's it?"

"What do you mean is that it? I kissed Mackenzie; Kyle's wife."

He heard an inpatient sigh on the other end from Dustin.

"For starters, you are looking at this wrong and I've already told you that. She is now a widow and it's been over a year. I think she's ready to decide that it's okay to move on and so should you."

"I know, but I'm more disappointed at how good it felt. I think deep down I was hoping we wouldn't have any kind of chemistry and we could laugh at it and put it behind us."

"I told you it wasn't going to work out like that. You are too deeply involved and there is no backing down from that. Did she slap you or scream at you? What happened?"

Trey exhaled thinking back to the heady kiss.

"She kissed me back and I'm telling you no woman has ever, ever made me feel the way I felt when I kissed her."

"That means something."

"Yeah, it means I'm stabbing my friend in the back."

"Kyle's gone Trey and you have to let that go. I know it seems odd that you would be attracted to her especially knowing who she is, but that won't make the fact that obviously you both are struggling with some pretty strong feelings for each other that you can't just walk away from. I'm not trying to throw you together, but I know you. You wouldn't do this lightly so it means something. You can't walk away from that. There is nothing sordid about the feelings that have developed between the two of you and whatever happened or will happen, you need to come out with the fellas tonight and get that chip off of your shoulder. You're thinking too hard about this and beating yourself up because you've fallen in love with a woman and that woman is Mackenzie. Stop thinking about it so much and meet us there. I'll give you an hour and if I don't see you, I'm coming to get you."

Trey knew he was right. He needed an outlet for the stress that was building up since he'd left Mackenzie standing in her living room looking desirous. A night out could be exactly what he needed to think through how to come back from what occurred.

"Yeah, I'll be there."

Dustin was probably right, Trey thought as he

headed in the direction of his shower. He needed to shake it off. He kissed her, it's done and he couldn't take it back, not that he even wanted to.

A night of drinking was exactly what he needed to clear his head. He was meeting them at a club to hear a band that had been traveling the country and getting rave reviews.

**

Mackenzie, Ava and a few of their friends walked into the night club and immediately joined in with the festive vibe. The band was playing and the place was packed. Luckily Ava had called ahead and reserved them a table since they also came to eat.

It wasn't until she got inside of the club that she realized it was the kind of outing she needed. She spent the time prior to meeting up with them trying to get her mind off of the kiss she and Trey shared, not because it was awful, but because it defied description. The way he made her feel from just one kiss scared her because she wanted more, but it wasn't meant to be. She needed to have an evening free of thoughts of Trey and she'd deal with what was happening between them another time.

After they were settled into their table she was finally relaxed and ready for a glass of wine.

"Damn, I want one of those!" Kelly exclaimed.

"Me too!" she heard Kelly's sister Kelsey add.

Everyone around the table turned to look in the direction both ladies were looking in.

"The military must be growing them in a field or

something. I've never seen so much alpha male-ness in one place at the same time in my life. The only one I know is Trey and I can't wait to find out who the other guys are assuming they are military like him. I'll take either one of them or maybe even all of them," Kelsey added.

Everyone laughed except for Mackenzie.

"They're all military," Ava explained.

Mackenzie locked eyes with Trey and the kiss they'd shared earlier flooded her mind. She wasn't expecting to run into him. Besides seeing him, her next thought was that he looked incredible dressed in all black looking like he just leaped off the pages of a men's fashion magazine. Kelsey was right and Trey fit the description of the perfect alpha male. He was sitting at a table with Dustin, Ivan and Cal, three of his business partners. She looked around and noticed they were not the only ones keeping an eye on the handsome four at the corner table. The women in the club were pointing and flirting just as they were.

"Do you see Trey?" Ava asked, pulling Mackenzie's attention away from ogling him.

"Yes, I see him."

"Did you know he and his friends were going to be here tonight?"

"No, I talked to him earlier today and he didn't mention anything about coming here. He did say he had plans tonight."

While Ava talked, she looked back over in Trey's direction and he was still staring at her as they once again locked eyes.

"I think we're about to have company," Kelsey exclaimed when Trey and Dustin headed in their direction. Mackenzie wasn't ready to be up close and personal with Trey in front of everyone so she decided to excuse herself to get some space between them.

"I'm going to go check the place out a little bit since everybody is dancing. Besides, it looks like it will take our waitress a while to get here to take our drink order and I want to grab a glass of wine. I'll be back in a few minutes."

She stood just as Trey and Dustin reached the table.

"Hi Kenzie," Trey said.

"Hi Trey. I was just about to find the ladies room. I'll be back," she said and rushed off before he could say anything else.

She needed to make a hasty exit before she said something stupid like admit to Trey that he looked sexy and that she couldn't stop thinking about him.

She didn't miss the many stares from the women in the club as he walked across the floor to them. He always garnered a lot of attention and strangely, a hint of jealousy creeped up. The distance will do her some good.

She didn't look back as she made her way through the crowd and realized there was more than one level. She took the steps to go one level up where she could hear music playing. When she reached the landing, she noticed that the second level had just as many people as the level below. Seeing the bar in the far corner, she made her way through the crowd.

"Can I buy you a drink?" a voice said from behind her.

"No thank you," she replied without turning around.

"Aw, come on. Be nice and let a gentleman buy you a drink. You sure are one beautiful woman, curvy in all the places I like."

"Thank you," Mackenzie said and hoped he'd walk away. Even with her back to him, she could smell the alcohol on his breath and it was strong.

"You could at least turn around and look at me so that we can get to know each other."

Mackenzie jumped when she felt his hand on her arm. She tried to move away, but he didn't release her. She didn't want to cause a scene, but he was making her nervous.

"Take your hand off of her or lose the use of it for the rest of your life," Trey said coming up beside her. She turned to see the grimace on his face that said he was ready to make his threat a reality. She also saw that the guy had no idea who he was dealing when he tried to come back at Trey. Big mistake, she thought noticing that Trey outmatched him in height and in weight.

"Unless this is your wife and I don't see a ring on her finger, back off buddy," the guy said and that made Trey step even closer.

Before Trey could react, the bartender intervened. He must have seen the look on Trey's face that shouted murder.

"Buddy, trust me when I say you don't want to piss

this guy off. You must be new around these parts if you don't know who you're talking to so my advice is take your drink and go on about your business or I'll have my guys help this guy toss you out and getting tossed out from the second level could be painful. From the look on this guy's face, I don't think he'll take the time to walk you back downstairs first."

The guy took a second look in Trey's direction and backed off.

"Whatever, I'm leaving. Your loss sweetheart," he said to her before walking off.

"Oh wow, all I said was I didn't want him to buy me a drink. Is this how aggressive men are these days? I guess this is what I've missed out on."

"He doesn't represent all men, trust me. That probably wasn't his first drink of the night and though it's not an excuse, alcohol probably had a little to do with his aggressiveness, but don't worry about it. I doubt if he gives you any more trouble."

"What are you doing up here? I left you downstairs to continue being ogled by every woman in this place. Does that happen everywhere you go?"

Trey wanted to lie and say no, but he knew she already knew that it did and saw first-hand herself before she walked away.

"It does, but I don't play into it, at least I haven't lately. My thoughts aren't on bedding every woman I come across. I'm looking for something more than that."

"You don't have to play anything down for me. I

know what they see."

He didn't want to discuss other women with her.

"Dance with me," he said taking her hand.

Without hesitation, Mackenzie followed him to the dance floor. When he turned around and pulled her close, she went into his arms and the last time they were this close was the kiss earlier.

"You look incredible."

"So do you," she responded.

Mackenzie was as nervous as a high school girl dancing with a high school crush.

"Imagine my surprise running into you here. I know you said you were going out with friends tonight, but I guess you never said where."

"You didn't either. Was this a last minute decision?"

"No, the guys and I had this planned out for about a week. Dustin wanted to hear this band everyone around the country is raving about. I was going to stay home, but I changed my mind and came out anyway."

"Ava planned this girl's night out for me so that I could get out and have some fun. They're all pushing me to live a little more and I guess this is their attempt and making sure I do."

"I saw you smiling across the room and it was good to see you having a good time."

Mackenzie looked around frantically afraid that someone would see them dancing close together."

"They're all downstairs."

"What?" she said looking back up at him.

"You're looking around to see if anyone will see us

dancing this close together and before you deny it, remember I've spent most of my life in special ops learning how to read people."

"Was I that obvious?"

"I don't want to make you uncomfortable if you'd prefer to go back downstairs. I can feel you stiffening in my arms. If I promise not to kiss you again will you relax and enjoy the dance," he said with a hint of humor to lighten the mood.

Mackenzie exhaled realizing she was going overboard. It's just a dance.

"I'm sorry. I don't know what it is about you, but just like earlier, I think we're setting ourselves up for something neither one of us wants or needs."

"Don't Mackenzie. Don't try to talk yourself or me out of the fact that we've suddenly found ourselves attracted to each other. I don't know about you, but I've been thinking about it and I think once we sit down and talk this out, I think it will be okay."

She was about to reply when the music was turned up louder.

"We can't Trey," Mackenzie whispered, hoping he could hear her over the loud music. If nothing else, perhaps he could read lips because his gaze was centered on her lips and the want she saw in his eyes was unmistakably a desire to kiss her.

"We can't what?" he asked without taking his gaze from her lips.

"What are we doing?"

"I think we're dancing."

"Is that all we're doing?"

"Is that all you want to do?"

"Trey?"

"What do you want me to say?"

"Truth," she replied quickly.

Trey moved close to her ear.

"Truth is you are all I think about and I can't seem to stop. It wasn't just the kiss because what I've been feeling started a few months ago."

"Perhaps it's the alcohol talking," she said.

"I haven't had anything to drink yet. My beer is still sitting on my table, so it's not the alcohol. It's me talking. Can you honestly say I haven't been on your mind at least since we kissed earlier? I'm not trying to press you into anything, but I think we need to talk about what's happening and figure out what to do. It's not going to just go away. What are you going to do? Go back to ignoring me?"

As soon as the words left his mouth he regretted them.

"I'm going to go back to the table to find Ava and the girls. You should probably go in search of your friends because I'm sure they're all wondering where you and I are."

Mackenzie pulled free of his embrace.

"Wait, Mackenzie."

"Don't say anything right now. What happened earlier cannot happen again. We shouldn't be doing this."

"Are you sorry I kissed you? I can't say that I'm sorry

at all. Don't feel bad or ashamed that you wanted or needed that."

"I can't with you."

Mackenzie turned and made her way through the crowd before Trey had an opportunity to respond. As she neared the table, she saw that Ava and the others were at the table ordering food. She took her seat and tried to join back in the fun.

"You were gone so long I started to send the forces out looking for you," Ava said.

"Oh, there is a level upstairs I discovered while walking around and I stayed to listen to a few songs before coming back down."

That was all she planned on sharing.

"Okay, we were talking about some gossip that's been spreading around the hospital."

Mackenzie smiled and joined in the conversation making sure to keep her back to the table where Trey sat and fought the temptation to turn around and look at him. Her struggle between wanting and not wanting Trey was as real as they come.

After a while of going between gossip and listening to the band, she couldn't fight the temptation to see what Trey was doing so she turned around and saw the guys still sitting at their table, but no Trey. He looked disappointed when she left him on the dance floor and no doubt his night had been ruined. She had stopped enjoying the evening and needed to make an exit herself. This craziness with Trey was impacting her every waking moment. She had no clue what to do about it.

"Ava, this has been fun, but I'm going to head out."

"Aw, already? You haven't danced or anything yet and the point of getting you out was to have some fun and to learn how to mingle with men again."

"Well let me learn how to mingle nice and slow and tonight is not going to be that night. I have a Kylie free night and I want to get home to do more than just sleep. Who knows when I'll have a baby free night again, so I'm going to catch up with you girls tomorrow. Thanks for getting me out of the house tonight. We'll have to do this again really soon. I did have fun and it was good to let down my hair for the night."

She nervously looked around again this time scanning the dance floor and back to the table where Trey sat.

"If you're looking for Trey, he left. I saw him walk out the door almost an hour ago."

"Oh, I was going to go over and say goodnight, but since he's gone I won't worry about it. It's odd that he didn't stop over here before he left. He probably left with a woman."

"I don't think so. Are you going to sit here next to me and act jealous and not expect me to react? We talked about this; stop fighting it and if Trey is what you want, no one needs to be all up in your business."

"There is no business to be all up in," she replied and smiled to let Ava know everything was alright.

Mackenzie grabbed her things and Ava got up to walk her out.

"I'm going to make sure you get to your car okay."

"You don't have to do that. I saw on our way in that there is security that escorts women to their cars so I'm going to get one of the guys to do that so that you aren't walking back here by yourself."

They hugged and Mackenzie went in search of an escort back to her car. After locating one, she walked a few steps ahead of him to her car and when she was safely inside, she waved to let him know she was okay and she drove in the direction of her home.

The night hadn't turned out the way she'd planned, hoping to get her mind off of Trey and there he stood, live and in sexy color and untouchable as far as she was concerned.

14

Trey slammed the door for the second time tonight. He'd once again made the connection between him and Mackenzie odd. If he had set out to ruin their friendship, he was doing a good job of it.

Nothing could have prepared him for the onslaught of salacious feelings he felt every time he was around her. He knew he shouldn't have pulled her into his arms again, but he'd been enraged when he saw some guys hand on her arm and he needed to calm down. He knew being able to concentrate on her would do that. Even that had turned out all wrong when the experience of earlier in the day had them feeling melancholy as they relived the event from earlier when they'd kissed. If she hadn't pulled away from him, he probably would have kissed her again. They were drawn to each other even if Mackenzie wanted to continue fighting it.

Trey wasn't planning on tempting her again. It was clear that nothing was going to work out well for them and he'd rather give up trying and not lose the friendship they had. She and Kylie meant everything to him.

When he decided to hang out with the guys at the club, he didn't expect to run into her and when he first set eyes on her, his heart felt like it was about to leap from his chest with overwhelming craving for her.

He wondered around his house still unable to sleep since his mind and body were still amped up, filled with thoughts of Mackenzie in that black dress. It covered every important part, but left a lot open for him to desire. When did he start seeing her this way? He never looked at her in any way other than a friendship way for all the years he'd known her. Now when he looked at her he saw a sexy, vibrant woman that he wanted to claim as his own, something he still needed to sort out. There were millions of women in the world and when he finally finds a connection with one that is probably a once in a lifetime one, it turns out to be Mackenzie.

He didn't know what he was supposed to do about the attraction. Should he fight it and walk away because of who she was and not want her? She was gorgeous, more beautiful than any woman he'd ever met and the only other woman in the world who he would choose over her would be Kelly Rowland, the singer who used to be in the group Destiny's Child because she and Mackenzie looked so much alike from their smooth brown skin, long black curly hair to their shapely, sexy bodies.

One thing was different about Mackenzie that he realized separated her from the way he would, in the past, lust after a woman; it wasn't just about how beautiful she was or how she'd look completely naked writhing around under him. He wanted all of her and no woman ever claimed that spot in his heart. In true disbelief, he couldn't believe that once he'd found the perfect woman for himself, she'd turn out to be the woman who was once married to his friend. She may be single now, but she was still once married to him and for that reason alone, she should be off limits.

Dustin continually telling him that he's dissecting the situation too much and thinking too hard on it hasn't helped him feel any better about it. Mackenzie was right; they needed to back up from what could be a train accident waiting to happen. He knew one way to try and get Mackenzie off of his mind and it was a phone call away. He needed a distraction and having a list of distractions was exactly what he needed to get over his desire for Mackenzie.

He reached for his phone to locate the number of a female he was casual friends with that he knew would give his body the relief it needed.

**

Mackenzie was about to drive into her driveway and surprised herself when she kept driving by without stopping. She wanted to go home, but the thought of going home to an empty house didn't appease her. It was getting close to midnight and she was still out driving around the streets of Monterey with no destination in mind.

Thinking about Trey, she knew she was playing a dangerous game. Would she feel that way if it were any man other than Trey? What kind of man is she supposed to be interested in now that she had to move on? Would a friend be off limits forever or is there a time when you have to say it's okay if that friend brings all the qualities that you would look for in a man? What were the dating rules? She didn't know.

Mackenzie knew that she had to do something. She couldn't continue to fight herself and to fight Trey forever. Her mind and body won't continue to survive the level of emotions she experienced every time she was in his presence. It's not just lust when it comes to him and she knew that. She was falling in love with him and that's not something she took lightly. She had only been in love once in her life and now that he's gone, she found herself at the precipice of that kind of love again. As a line from one of her favorite songs says, it can't be wrong when it feels so right.

Before she was able to figure out where she was, Mackenzie found herself pulling into Trey's street with his house in her view.

**

Trey jumped when his doorbell sounded throughout the house, knowing that the hour was late and he wasn't expecting anyone.

He grabbed his sweatpants from the foot of the bed where he laid them when he had finally decided to call it a night. He slept in the buff, but didn't want to answer his door that way. He had a time or two in the past when he was expecting a woman and wanted her to know exactly what was on the menu, but that wasn't the case tonight. Who would be dropping by this late, he thought? He heard the bell again and rushed to see who it was.

He was shocked to see from the camera that pointed to the front of his house that on the other side of the door stood Mackenzie. He turned off the alarm and snatched the door opened, hoping there was nothing wrong.

"Kenzie, are you alright?"

When she looked up at him, he knew that her visit at this hour had nothing to do with any crisis other than the same one he was dealing with when it came to her.

"I was on my way home and I ended up on your street. I'm sorry if I'm interrupting anything. I can leave if I am."

"What would you be interrupting?"

"Oh, I don't know, something," she said, with a questionable look on her face.

He caught on.

"There is nobody here Kenzie; I'm alone."

"Oh, okay," she replied nervously.

He liked that she looked relieved and a little jealous. Mackenzie thought he had a woman in his house and yet she came by anyway.

"Do you want to come in or do you want me to come out to talk?"

He was giving her an out.

"Do you mind if I come in?"

"You're always welcome here," he said, moving to the side to let her in.

Mackenzie walked by Trey into his living room and tried to catch her breath after seeing him shirtless. She'd seen him like that many times before when he would be working outdoors on his yard, her yard or her in-laws' yard, but seeing him now in that half sleep, half-awake look with only a pair of gym pants riding low on his toned hips had her thinking she should have asked him to step outside. A saucy chill crept up her spine as heat engulfed her. She was beyond enamored.

After she entered the living room and took a seat, Mackenzie nervously fumbled with her keys as she watched Trey stand at the door without moving. She was afraid to look at him and she had no clue of what to say. She had nothing planned when she showed up at his house other than she felt the need to see him, to be close to him.

When she finally looked at him, he looked at her perplexed and she understood. She was continually pushing him away from her, but here she sat in his living room in the middle of the night. He wasn't the only one confused.

"I guess you're wondering why I'm here?"

"You don't need a reason to come to my house and you can do so at any time, but I will say you have me curious."

"Tonight," she said.

"What about tonight?"

"This is hard for me Trey. I don't know what to do about the thoughts of you that I can't get out of my head. I know I keep pushing you away and that's because having feelings for you isn't easy for me and I know it's not easy for you either."

"Kenzie, one thing I know is that we can't keep going around and around like this. I won't apologize anymore for the fact that I have feelings for you and I want more than just a friendship with you. I can see the repercussions of what could happen if we move forward with anything, but I also see something beautiful that I've never had before and I can't fight the fact that I want that and I want that with you. Yes, I know who you are and how strange this is to you, but is it really strange? I've never looked at you before the way I look at you now. I've never disrespected him like that by secretly lusting after you. These feelings grew over the last few months and I think it's okay to feel this way. I think that he has brought us together knowing that I would always look out for you and Kylie and what's happening between us is imminent. I don't, however, want to put you in a compromising position to struggle with whether this is right or wrong. If what you want is for us to remain friends, I will respect that and back off. Your friendship means more to me than anything and I don't want anything to impact that."

"I thought about these same things on my way over here tonight. I was hesitant at first because I thought maybe I'd get here and you would have a woman over here. I can't begin to tell you how jealous I was thinking that. All I could envision was you touching and kissing a woman and that terrified me. I didn't want to send you into the arms of another woman tonight out of frustration over what's happening or not happening between us."

Trey smiled and came closer into the room.

"There is no other woman and I will admit that the thought crossed my mind to call one to try and help me wipe my desirous thoughts of you from my mind and in the end, I couldn't make that call because I don't want another woman. I want you."

"I want you too Trey."

"Are you sure?" he asked.

"I've never been surer."

"Come here Kenzie."

Mackenzie stood and slowly walked over to him. When he didn't reach out for her to pull her into his arms, she understood that any step forward from this point on would have to be hers. Not taking her eyes off of his, she reached up and ran her hands over his muscled chest and watched the play of emotions on his face as he fought to react.

"Right or wrong, you are who I want," she said. She put any reservations she had to the side. She was here, in his house and there was no backing down now.

To show him that she was hesitant, she looked up at him right before leaning forward and placing a soft kiss on one side of his chest and then the other, taking in his masculine scent. Being this bold was never her forte, but tonight she was feeling daring. She leaned further up and snaked her tongue out and licked across the base of his neck where it met his collarbone, paying special attention to the vein that now stood out as he tried to contain his desire to reach out and pull her to him. She smiled at his level of control and was hoping to break through that barrier.

Trey was on the verge of losing his mind the moment her tongue touched him. When she reached his neck, he heard himself groan out his approval of her aggressiveness. He needed whatever they were about to do to be about her and not about him so he would let her take what she needed. He wanted her to know that this was more than just intimacy for him if they were going to continue.

"Kenzie, this isn't something casual for me and it's important to me that you understand that. There is more than a powerful sexual attraction going on between us and though I want to indulge more than you know, I can't have a casual one-night stand with you and I don't care how desperate I am for you right now, I can take an extremely cold shower and go to bed if I need to. I know the hour is late and the sexual tension in this room could set this place on fire, so think through what you want with me. If we're not on the same page, this could be disastrous in the end."

Mackenzie didn't speak. She moved close enough that there was no room between their bodies. She pressed up against him and discovered his need for her was rock hard, long and moving against her stomach.

She leaned up as far as she could on her the tips of her toes in her five inch heels, inviting him to come closer and see how serious she was.

Trey got her message and leaned down while lifting her chin up to meet her for the kiss, making sure there was no urgency to it. He preferred nice and slow so that she felt every bit of the desire and the rush of heat flowing from him to her.

He captured her lips taking first the bottom and then the top savoring her mouth, zestfully sampling first softly and then getting a little more intense, paying homage to her mouth. When Mackenzie opened her lips to give him full access, he dived in intoxicated by the potent taste of her, with his mind spinning into realms of ecstasy he never knew existed. When she moaned into his mouth, he inhaled her breath taking in the sweet scent of her as his body raged out of control with an eagerness to take her standing right in the middle of his living room.

Getting Mackenzie to his bed was the only thing on his mind as he pulled back from the kiss to look down at her. She had a sensual glow on her face that told him that she wanted him as much as he wanted her and now wasn't the time for him to second guess the decision to make love to her. If this wasn't the right thing to do, he was more than willing to apologize to any and every one another time, but tonight, he was going to give them both the relief they longed for.

Trey reached down and grabbed Mackenzie's legs, sliding her dress up her thighs until he could open them wide enough to wrap them snuggly around his hips. As she held on to his shoulders, he captured her lips again and brought her body close enough for him to move her around on his erection giving her a taste of what she was in for. When she started grinding her own hips against him, he was done for.

"I have you in my arms still trying to decipher if this is real or a dream and in a few seconds, I'm going to head for the steps that will take us up to my room. I'm giving you an out here to change your mind right now if you're not sure about what we're about to do. I want you so damn bad and the minute we get up there and I get you anywhere near a bed, I intend to have you. Let me know right now if there is any reluctance or reservation right now and we'll stop and try our best to go back to what we were before you showed up here."

Mackenzie didn't have to think because if she did, she would try and talk herself out of what her mind and body wanted. Tonight she wanted to feel wanted, needed and loved and she knew on the ride to his house that she would find it in his arms and that's all she wanted to do; be in his arms making love to him.

She leaned back to look him square in the eyes, never ceasing the movements of her hips on his pulsing manhood which appeared to grow in length and width the more she moved across his hips.

"Damn!" he shouted when he felt like he body was already prepared to quake.

"I know, so can we get to a bed and stop so much talking. I'm not changing my mind after I've gotten to this point. No more fight it and tonight, what I need is you," she uttered before taking his mouth in a searing kiss, letting him know that any thoughts of them not going up to his room should be wiped clean from his mind.

Trey didn't need any more of an invitation than that. He held on to her as he turned toward the stairs while savoring her lips over and over giving her a prelude to what he intended to do to her body.

Mackenzie relished in the feel of Trey's hard body against hers. Thankfully he was shirtless and she could rub her hands all over his hardened body. She ran her hands over his arms, up and around to his back before bringing her hands forward and planting them on his hard-rock chest. She slid them down further to his abs and a chill went through her with the realization that she would soon be able to slide her hands further down his body once they were both naked.

"I'm starving for you," she heard him say the moment they passed through the doorway to his bedroom.

She'd been to his house before, but never up to top level. Still in his arms, she looked around the room at its massive size and at the large bed that sat in the middle of the room. She turned her eyes back to Trey as he walked them to his bed and slowly laid her down on it while following her down.

"Are you sure Kenzie?" he asked again, giving her a chance to stop them before they went past the point of no return.

"I'm more than sure. Like you, I've been thinking about you a lot and there is no place I'd rather be than right here with you."

"That's good to hear because ever since I saw you at the club in this black dress, I've been wondering what you'd look like with it off."

"Then why don't you take a look and see," she uttered in a sexy voice laced with essential need.

Trey didn't need a second invitation. He leaned back and without taking his eyes off of hers, he reached to her side and untied the wrap dress which fell open, flat on the bed. He thought he'd died and gone to heaven the moment his eyes roamed over her beautiful, well-toned body."

"You are truly beautiful."

Before Mackenzie could respond, Trey leaned forward and placed an open mouth kiss right below her breast.

Mackenzie almost leaped off of the bed when she felt his tongue make a trail from under her breast to down around her stomach. She felt his large hands caress her outer thighs before traveling inward using them to spread her legs open. Before she could assess what his next move would be, she felt his hands travel up her body on both sides until his hands reached over her breasts to caress her cleavage. After making small circles with his fingers, he used his hands to remove the front clasp that kept him from his prize. As soon as the cups to her bra fell away freeing her globes, she watched him move in slow motion, leaning down taking first one hard pebbled nipple into his mouth and teasing it to an even harder peak before moving on to the other, giving it equal attention. The sight of him making love to her breasts already had her on the brink filling her heart and body's desires.

Trey was mesmerized by Mackenzie's luscious body and knew that he needed to get in her body sooner rather than later. He stopped his caresses when he knew it was time to divest her of every stitch of clothing she had on. First he removed the purse she still hand in her hand and tossed it to the floor. He then pulled her up until she was sitting so that he could remove the dress and bra he'd just removed. He didn't look where those had landed as he tossed them behind him. He slid his hands down her long, toned legs until he reached her shoe clad feet. Luckily they easily slid from her feet and he let them join her clothing which was some place on the floor as well. The last bit of clothing that separated him from having her completely bare before him was now in his grasp as he slid the barely there, thin black lace thong panties down and off of her bottled shaped hips.

Now that he had her completely naked before him, he lifted her up again and this time placed her at the head of the bed while he removed his sweat pants, the only piece of clothing he had on.

Mackenzie reached over toward him.

"I wanted to take those off of you," she said.

"Next time I will let you, but right now, if you touch me, I might burst into flames."

When Mackenzie smiled at him, he knew that making love to her tonight was what he was supposed to do. He could see the passionate stare coming from her and knew that it matched his. After reaching into his night stand for protection, he joined her on the bed.

"I need to make a confession," he said.

"Okay," she replied breathlessly.

Mackenzie didn't know what the confession was, but she hoped it wasn't that he was having second thoughts.

"I have been dreaming about being here with you just like this and taking my time savoring every part of your body until I'd driven you crazy, but now that you're here, I don't think I can take my time because I'm not sure I'd last through the heart attack I'd give myself with the sheer torture of taking my time. I want and need to be inside of you, but I promise, there will be time for more enjoyment and foreplay if that's what you want and need."

Mackenzie knew she didn't need all that; at least not right now.

"What I need right now is you, inside me."

Trey didn't hesitate to undo the wrapper and covered his already painfully hard member. He then slid between her legs pulling them up so that they encased his hips. Without any more words, he leaned down and once again brought their lips together as he reached down between them to test her readiness for him. When he touched her and a pool of moisture greeted his finger, he knew she was more than ready for him.

Mackenzie arched off of the bed the minute his fingers touched her intimately and she needed him to get inside of her. To prove her point, she ground her hips up toward him while delighting in the passionate, intoxicating kiss that dazzled every fiber of her being.

When Trey removed his fingers, the movement of her hips caused his erection to press long and hard against her middle and she could feel an excitement building up inside of her in anticipation of what he would feel like the minute he entered her. Tonight she was his and whatever he wanted to do to pleasure them both, she was ready for.

"Are you ready for me?" he whispered in her ear as he leaned down into the area between her shoulder and her ear.

Mackenzie was more than ready and she could feel just how ready he was for her.

"Yes and I can feel you," she said moving under him to let him know her desire was growing.

When Trey reached down to spread her legs a little wider, she felt the tip of him at her entrance and sighed in anticipation. She felt him slide into her a little at a time, now feeling for herself how massive he was. Though she was far from a virgin, his solid hardness made slow controlled movements into her body. She felt a little pain, but knew the end result would be well worth any pain his size may cause. Excitement started to build when she realized he was taking his time so that he wouldn't hurt her, but she needed more and she needed it now.

"I know why you're going slowly, but you won't hurt me. I need you," Mackenzie whispered in his ear. "I can tell by the way you're gritting your teeth that you're trying to hold back, but don't."

To show Trey she meant business, Mackenzie pushed her hips up and into him causing him to thrust deep into her body with one long thrust until he was completed sated in her body, causing them both to exhale with exhilaration.

"You're going to kill me Kenzie," he uttered through clinched teeth.

"I know the feeling and trust me the feeling is great," she admitted. Before she could say anything else, Trey slid out of her body before surging back in again and again bringing them both to the brink each time he entered her.

Mackenzie wrapped her legs even tighter around his waist as Trey used strong, solid, deep thrusts to bring her to the edge sooner than she wanted, but the feeling was too great to fight as the desire to let go grew. She used all of the energy she could muster to match him stroke for stroke drawing from him all that he had to give her. When she felt him moving his hips in a circular motion that caused him to hit every spot that made her body shiver, she screamed when an orgasm tore through her, causing her to gasp and grind her hips even harder into him.

"That's it, take what you need from me!" he shouted before he too joined her in sensual bliss as pleasure ripped through ever muscle in his body, shattering his façade' into a million pieces. He groaned and she moaned as they rocked together to the sounds of him going in and out of her slippery folds, made even wetter when he felt her again reach her peak before the waves of another orgasm crashed into her, sending her on another upward spiral to another powerful explosion.

"Trey!" she screamed.

"I'm right here with you baby," he responded.

Trey didn't stop as he leaned down to lick and nibble on her neck and then traveling down her neck to her breasts, leaving a wet path down her body. As her body calmed, he slowed his ministrations in and out of her body while still placing soft kissing over her over-sensitized body.

Mackenzie wasn't sure how much time had passed before her body finally relaxed from the rollercoaster ride Trey had just taken her on.

"That was amazing," she said when she was able to catch her breath.

Trey's sentiment matched hers.

"Yes it was and as far as I'm concerned we've just begun."

As he leaned down to kiss her once more, Mackenzie's eyes widened when she felt him grow hard again while he was still snug within her body.

"I see you're ready to begin again. Are you sure you don't want to catch your breath and maybe a nap first?"

Trey moved around inside of her body showing her that this wasn't the time for a break or a nap.

Mackenzie smiled and followed his lead and joined in the race to pleasure again.

15

Mackenzie woke to bright sunlight shining on her face, making her squint as she opened her eyes. A few minutes went by before realization set in and she remembered where she was; in bed with Trey. The memory of the night before poured in and flashed in her mind as images of kissing Trey, making love to Trey and him devouring every part of her body. As good as it felt, at the moment all she felt was embarrassment and shame knowing she wanted him as much as she did and at the same time, wishing that she didn't.

She hated that she woke with doubt on her mind, but she couldn't shake it. In the light of day, she'd have to look him in the face and that would be no easy task. He was Trey, she thought.

Mackenzie felt an urgency to get into her own space and avoid the morning after discussion. She needed to go.

She moved slightly and felt the hardness of Trey's arm which was draped over her and lay in front of her on the bed right next to her naked breast. She needed to move and do so before he woke up and they ended up talking about what she didn't want to talk about.

She slid forward on the bed as lightly as she could, trying not to wake him. When she finally made it where her feet reached the floor, she went in search of her clothes. She knew they were scattered across the room as more images flooded her mind of Trey slowly removing every stitch the night before without hesitation and then flinging clothing about the room where neither of them cared where it landed. All they wanted was to get each other naked and satisfy the sexual tension that had been surrounding them for weeks.

Feeling ashamed like never before, Mackenzie grabbed first her panties and decided against slipping them on and decided instead to slip them in her bag which sat on a chair near the door. She saw the dress she'd worn for her ladies night out and quickly slipped it on, retying it at the waist. As soon as she saw her bra which had somehow landed on the door handle, she felt Trey stirring in the bed. She hoped he was just tossing and wouldn't wake. She stood still until she heard silence again and grabbed for the bra.

"Mackenzie, are you going to leave without saying anything?"

Trey slid out of the bed and grabbed the sweatpants from the bedside chair, pulling the string at the waist to pull them tight around his hips.

Mackenzie didn't respond as she continued to dress, unable to turn and look him in the face. She slipped her feet in her heels and exhaled keeping her eyes on the floor.

"You're not going to talk to me at all or perhaps ever again? I assume this is the part where regret over the night before sets in and you're disappointed that you made the trip to my house, that you rang my bell and that I opened the door. Is there any part of last night that you're not feeling bad about?"

Mackenzie didn't move and knew that the moment he walked over to her and stood in front of her, she wasn't going to get out of there as easily as she hoped. She was going to have to face it and now seemed like as good a time as any.

"The way I'm feeling right now isn't because of you Trey; it's because I made a choice last night that I now have to deal with."

"There was nothing wrong with the choice you made."

She wasn't sure if he remembered being in the same bed with her last night the way she remembered it.

"Everything is wrong with what happened last night. It never, ever should have happened and you know that just as I do. It doesn't matter how much I wanted you or how much you wanted me, we were wrong for what we did and now what are we supposed to do? We crossed a line last night and it was a line neither of us should have ever crossed and now we can't go back to a point where this didn't happen."

Trey stooped down and used his finger to lift Mackenzie's chin so that they were looking at each other. He knew that she was purposely trying to avoid looking at him, but he wanted her to know that he had no regrets and he needed her to see it in his face.

"I know where you're going with this and I can respect the feelings you have, but don't think I'm going to join you on the regret train because I don't feel remorse about anything we did. I can't say it hasn't been a struggle for me wanting you and feeling like I shouldn't because of the connection we share."

"The connection that you speak of is more than enough reason for us to have let leveler heads prevail and walk away from this. I shouldn't have come here last night and you shouldn't have let me in. We both knew what was going to happen and as much as I tried to halt my steps to your house, something else came over me. Thoughts of you have been haunting me for a while and I don't want you to think I'm saying haunting as if I'm referring to something frightening. I haven't been able to sleep because I think of you constantly. When I see you I get nervous and my palms get sweaty like a teenage girl. There is something I feel for you that I can't explain and I don't know if I want to. All I know is that what happened between us should not have happened and now things will change because of it and that change may not be a good one."

"Why would things have to change, at least in a negative way? You slipping out without saying anything wasn't going to help anything. If you're having issues with what happened, we need to talk about it and not let it sit around like an elephant in the room every time we see each other. Last night happened because we both wanted it to, that is until you woke up this morning and thought too much about it."

"I can't help how I'm feeling right now. A lot of things come to life in the light of day."

"So what happens now? You'll see me and we'll act as if last night didn't happen? Was this a one-time thing and we're never to speak of it again? I don't know about you, but I'm hoping this wasn't a one-time thing and that you and I can explore more of what we're feeling. I know that I'm not interested in sharing my bed with you this one-time as if I don't want more and that more I'm speaking of is not about sex or making love, but it's about exploring what we could possibly have together."

Mackenzie knew she couldn't have this conversation with him. This was bad, she thought, really bad and right now she needed to get out and get some fresh air so that she could think through what was next. She couldn't do that with him standing in front of her looking all yummy and naughty and she really wished he'd put on a shirt. Her will-power was taking a serious hit and she was going to lose if she didn't get out now.

"I can't do this right now Trey; I just can't. There are others to think about besides you and me and the fact that we have an attraction that won't go away. What do you think Kyle's family will think if they knew what we did? Don't you think they'd feel like you and I betrayed Kyle in some way? That we are betraying them? Maybe they'll think you and I had something going on before all of this happened to Kyle?"

Mackenzie's last statement took him by surprise. He would never, ever have betrayed his friend in such a way and even though he always thought that she was nice, he knew that she was perfect for Kyle and he never, ever entertained thoughts about her in any other kind of way. Her words were crushing him. He knew she wasn't trying to be hateful, but that's what she was doing to justify her actions.

"Is that really what you're worried about? What someone else would think? You and I know the truth and that should be enough. Perhaps you should leave if somewhere in the back of your mind, the only thing that came out of the time we spent together is what someone else thinks we may or may not have been doing while Kyle was alive and you should give his family more credit than that. They know and love you and they know me and love me like a son. I believe that if they knew that you and I were developing feelings for each other, I don't think any of them would think that this could have started before Kyle's death. You know what, I change my mind about regretting last night because I do have one small regret and that is that the night we spent together, which was incredible in my book, made you come out of it and into the next day with nothing but negative thoughts. I'm sorry you feel the way you do, but don't expect me to join you in that circle. I care a great deal about you and if you're more worried about everyone else instead of you and I at this point, then you're right, it's time for you to leave."

Mackenzie looked at Trey and saw the hurt she'd caused and she wanted to apologize, but didn't think he'd want to hear it. She knew that she had to think of more than just their desire for each other and she had to walk away. Without saying another word, she left the bedroom and went straight for the front door and left without looking back.

When she reached her car, she put the key in and as she backed out of his driveway, she wondered if he was still standing there looking hurt. Before she pulled away, she looked up at his door and noticed that he'd shut it and she was sure that meant he'd also shut her out. It was for the best and hopefully they could both forget the night even happened.

16

"Dr. Ellis, you sure are looking mighty tired this morning. I guess someone isn't accustomed to being out drinking and having a good time on a work night," Ava said jokingly, knowing Mackenzie only had a few sips of her wine.

Mackenzie tried to stifle the yarn that escaped, but couldn't. She wasn't just tired, she was exhausted and it had nothing to do with the ladies night out.

"I thought coming in at three in the afternoon instead of eight in the morning was a good idea and I'd have the extra time to sleep before coming in. I'm glad I don't have any scheduled surgeries today because I can't stop yawning."

"Don't be yawning all over your patients today because you were out partying sort of late. I say sort of because you left earlier than I thought you would. I hope you took advantage of your baby free night."

Mackenzie didn't respond out loud, but to herself,

she knew she had done just that.

After she left Trey's house, she tried to go home to get some sleep before work, but couldn't. She called Kyle's parents to check on Kylie and could hear her laughing in the background. She didn't want to disturb whatever fun Kylie was engaged in so she told them she'd be by to pick her up after her shift at the hospital ended that night.

She showered, read through some mail that had been piling up and tried to catch a nap. Each time she closed her eyes, she saw Trey, naked making love to her, taking her higher and higher. Then she saw images of him under her in the heat of passion and her traitorous body tingled at the remembrance of how during either their second or third time, he'd let her take control of the love making and she remember being on top as he surrendered to her while they both raced toward their mutual satisfaction.

Her thoughts then turned to how their morning conversation had ended and the hurt she'd seen on his face. It wasn't his fault that she'd taken the drive over to his house after she left the club telling her friends she was headed home.

"It was a fun night, I will give you that. I had never been to that spot before and I couldn't believe the crowd. I'm wondering why that was your first time taking me there since it looks like it's the hottest spot in town."

"Girl, please stop playing with me. I'm always trying to get you to go out someplace with me and you're always declining with one excuse after another. Kylie is almost a year old and this is the first time you've been out since before you were pregnant with her and don't blame it on me. You know I love hanging out during my downtime. After days in this place, you have to get out and shake off what we see in this hospital every day. Did you go home and go to bed because you are yawning like you were up all night long looking over work as I know you have a terrible habit of doing?"

Mackenzie could usually count on telling Ava everything that was going on with her, but her night before needed to stay a secret. She was too ashamed for anyone to know that in her time of weakness, she had turned to Trey.

"I, um, I took a shower and went to bed. I was exhausted and besides, I didn't take any work home with me. I left all of my paperwork with one of the residents to get in order and prepare notes for me to read over today. I'm finally making use of all the help I have around this place."

"Enough work talk. Are we going to talk about the elephant in this conversation?" Ava asked.

Mackenzie tried to look befuddled.

"What elephant?"

"Trey. I saw the way you looked at him and I'm no fool; I saw the way he looked at you too.

"Don't try it Ava. I know we've talked about this and I told you, yes, Trey is handsome, but there is nothing there."

"Are you saying that to convince me or to convince

you because if it's for me, it's falling on deaf ears? I'm not saying you're in love with Trey, but there is something between the two of you that both of you are fighting and you need to stop denying it and go with it. There is nothing wrong if you and Trey find that there is more to you than just friendship."

"I can't with him Ava, and you know that. Don't you think it would be weird?"

Mackenzie asked for more than one obvious reason. She wanted to hear from someone else if it would be out of order for her to think that she and Trey could have anything more than friendship. Right now even that was in question after the night before and the intense morning after talk in his bedroom."

"You're thinking too hard if you think it would be weird. Are you asking because you do have feelings for him?"

"That's nonsense and you know it," she lied.

"If you say so," Ava added.

"I have rounds so I'm going to get going. Can you hand me my IPad from over there on the desk?"

Ava turned to grab it as another doctor walked by and greeted Mackenzie. She turned hearing him call her name and when she turned back around to Ava, there was a stunned look on her friends face.

"What's wrong with you?"

"What is that?" Ava asked.

Mackenzie, looking confused had no idea what she was making reference to.

"What's what?" she asked.

"That? On your neck? Is that a hickey I see? Wait, come here so that I can see that."

Mackenzie's nerves ramped up as she rubbed the area that Ava was pointing to. There was a little pain there and she knew that there was a possibility that with all the licking and sucking she and Trey had been doing the night before, that he may have left a mark or two. She remembered how he focused on her neck when he realized it was an erogenous zone for her. It felt so good at the time that she didn't think that the amorous night they'd shared could have left signs on parts of her body that were visible to anyone else. She did notice a few places on his chest that showed signs of the extra attention she'd paid to sucking on his pecks.

"No, it's not a hickey."

"Lie," Ava retorted.

Mackenzie tried to play it off as she reached for the IPad that Ava was holding out. Just before she was able to get her grip on it, Ava pulled it back.

"Oh, no you don't, not this time. I know exactly what that is and you are going to tell me what gives and I don't care what rounds you need to make."

"Ava, stop playing around. I'm already late for rounds and I just told you it's nothing."

"Is this why you're not interested in Trey? You've been seeing someone and haven't told me, your best friend about it? Are you serious right now?" she asked questionably.

Mackenzie knew it was time to walk away.

"I'm not seeing anyone and I told you it's nothing so give me my IPad so I can get to rounds girl," she said humorously trying to throw Ava off the conversation.

Mackenzie reached for it again and this time Ava pulled her close to get a closer look. She tried to pull away, but Ava was intent on checking it out for herself, up close and personal.

"You are going to stand in my face and lie to me. Are you serious right now?"

Ava leaned in close so that no one walking by could hear her.

"Keep your voice down," Mackenzie exclaimed calmly.

Ava then whispered.

"Someone has been sucking on your neck and I'm sure it's not something Kylie has done. Girl, I haven't seen a hickey like that since my college years so that must have been some fun you had."

Mackenzie was embarrassed.

"Stop it Ava and not now," she whispered, looking around to be sure no one else was around.

"Wait one minute!" Ava shouted and then covered her mouth before pulling Mackenzie into the empty file room behind them.

When they were inside, Ava shut the door and placed her hands on her hips while blocking the door to prevent Mackenzie from escaping. She smiled a sinister grin.

"You are going to spill and I don't care if you miss rounds for the rest of the day and anything else you have going on. I know for a fact you did not have that mark on your neck last night when we went out. The dress you had on last night had skinny straps and your neck was out so I would have seen that especially since I spotted it so easily even with your hospital coat on, so spill and don't try lying. Who the hell did you go see after you left the club last night or sometime this morning and why didn't you tell me you were seeing someone? All this time I was thinking you were secretly pining for Trey and you have been getting some on the side."

Mackenzie's nerves were frazzled and without thinking, she started pacing not sure how much to tell Ava without her freaking out. She needed an out.

"This is not the time for this Ava, especially not here at work where anyone could hear us and not to mention, I told you I have rounds, so let's do this after we're off and I promise I'll tell you everything, just not right now. I need to go to my office to see if I have a shirt that will cover up my neck I can wear under my scrubs."

She watched a show of emotion on Ava's face as she thought about the compromise and hoped she'd go for it.

"So it is a hickey? Ooh, girl I can't believe you would keep something this juicy from me. Give me a little something for now and we can pick the rest up later. Come on, it's me. You know your secret is safe with me so spill."

Mackenzie thought about it as she moved around

Ava and opened the door right after she grabbed the IPad from her hands. Before leaving out and without turning around to see the look on Ava's face, she gave her the little bit of information she asked for. She knew if she could trust anyone, she could trust Ava.

"It was Trey who put the mark there."

Mackenzie didn't wait around to see the expression on Ava's face and hoped she didn't leave her friend in the state of having a heart attack because she knew it was big news. She walked out in search of the other doctors and realized she actually felt better telling someone that something had happened between them and later, she'd lay it all out for Ava and find out if she's right to feel like she made a mistake.

17

Trey walked into his office in a foul mood and the guys around him glared at him as he walked by without even a slight greeting, went into his office and slammed the door. The minute the door was shut and rattled, he knew the door would soon open with one of the guys questioning him about his mood. Before he could get settled behind his desk to go through the mounds of papers, his office door opened and in walked Dustin. He looked up at him and then looked down at the papers as if he were trying to figure out a way to work his way through them.

"What gives Trey?"

"Nothing, I'm just having one of those mornings."

"Anything you want get off your chest? We have a lot to do today and it may be hard to do and work together if one of us has a chip on his shoulder and by one of us

I mean you."

Trey hated that the last words he'd had with Mackenzie was impacting his mood for the day. He told her he cared about her and the only response was that she was concerned about what others will think about the two of them. He was in love with her and he wondered what she would have done if he'd told her that. She probably would have packed up and left town again. He couldn't shake the horrible way her words had him feeling, but his friends didn't deserve his attitude.

"No, I'm good, so what's on tap for today?"

Dustin looked at him not sure he believed him, but he had a feeling he should let it go.

"Calvin and Ivan are putting in the weapons shelter underground today and we'll start wiring the war room today making it sound proof for anyone in the outer office to hear what we discuss in that room. You know Lincoln lives and breathes all this new spy technology and I know he wanted to go over a few things with you about what he's been able to secure. You up for that?"

"Yeah, I'm good."

"Whatever it is, shake it off and if it has anything to do with Mackenzie Ellis, you knew going in that things may not pan out the way you wanted."

Trey looked up at him as he leaned back in his seat.

"I know," was all he could think to say in response.

Dustin couldn't let the conversation end like that seeing that Trey was clearly in pain about something.

"What did you do Trey? I know what I'm thinking

168

you did, but I'm wondering if that's it."

Trey didn't respond and he knew the look on his face spoke volumes.

"It turned out bad huh?"

"Well, it started out great, but the next day, in the light of day, it turned bad, really bad. She's regretting it like you wouldn't believe and me, I am ecstatic because I'm in love with her and I'm not sure I have a right to be. She hit me with all of her regret."

"Do you share in her regret?"

"Hell no! I am in love with her Dustin, but today I realized we'll never be able to have anything more than what we shared last night because no matter how hard we try or how hard I may try, I don't think we can have anything. I loved him like a brother and she made me feel like I betrayed my love and friendship for him by loving her. I didn't set out to have these feelings for her and I right now I wished I didn't have them. I wanted her so damned bad that I let that cloud my judgement. I should have known she would feel this way."

"You couldn't have predicted that. She probably hadn't until after the fact."

"I hear you, but what the hell was I thinking making love to her?"

Dustin came closer and sat at the chair in front of his desk and he knew he was in for a speech. Dustin was the level head of the group, the big thinker and Trey trusted his judgement.

"You were thinking that after the tragedy that you both went through and yes I meant to say both because we know how much she loved Kyle and you loved him also, you found a path that led you to her. You were there for her through a rough time and I know you told me that you were afraid that she wouldn't make it through a broken heart and if it wasn't for Kylie, maybe she would not have, but either way, you were the friend she needed. That friendship turned into something more that I'm sure neither of you planned or expected, but it happened. Don't be upset with her for regretting whatever happened with the two of you, but you need to let her deal with this while still being her friend, if you can find your way back to that."

"I get the feeling things are going to be awkward and if she wants me to forget we made love last night, I can't do that. I will give her the space she needs and if she wants to walk away from me and what I think we can have, I have to let her because I love and respect her that much and I want her to be happy. I don't want to be the cause of any unhappiness especially if it's because she thinks we did something wrong."

"It wasn't wrong Trey, but neither of you may have been ready for the repercussions of what you did, so let her work it out and in the meantime, we have work to do. Lincoln's waiting for you and I'm joining Ivan and Calvin downstairs. Shake it off, but don't give up. Give her some time."

"I hear you and I appreciate it, oh wise one," Trey joked, feeling a little of the weight lifted.

"Yeah, yeah, whatever. What can I say, the women love me and it's my duty to oblige them all."

Trey laughed so hard he almost toppled backwards out of his chair. That caused both of them to laugh as the mood lightened and he got up to follow Dustin out of the room where they ran into a curious Ivan.

"See, I told you all he needed was a few minutes on the Dustin couch and you be less hulk-ish," Lincoln said to Ivan.

"What are you fools talking about?" Dustin asked.

"I'm not paying them any mind, but you do have a way of psychoanalyzing us all through our problems," Cal added.

"Yeah, I know his babble got me through my time overseas. The stuff that comes out of his mouth is better than any drug or medication around!" Ivan chimed.

"Shut up before I take my gun out and shoot all of you. We've got business to take care of and sometime before this week is out, we need to hire two office assistants who we need to vet to be sure they'll understand what we plan to do here at Game Changers."

"I have the perfect person to start out with," Lincoln added. "I worked with her at the secret service and I mentioned to her that we were opening up a security and private investigations business and she said she was looking for something new where she could stay in one place more often than she did working for the secret service. She's also been looking to relocate and I told her I would pass her bio on to you guys and if it helps any, I would vouch for her any day. She has the highest level of security clearance and she has a husband who's a doctor and I told her if she was interested in the job if offered, that I was sure he'd be able to get a job with his background in cardiology."

"Hey, I don't need to check out her bio and references as long as you're good with her and I think I speak for us all when I say, we're good with her," Dustin said.

"Me too," Calvin added.

After each guy agreed with Lincoln's choice, he told them he'd give her a call and see when she'd like to make her move. They weren't planning to have everything up and running for a few months while they got all their ducks in a row.

Trey tried to pay attention while his mind drifted to thoughts of Mackenzie and their night of passion. It didn't matter to him how regretful she was about their night together, he knew he would never forget it. He'd been with his share of women before, but nothing had felt as good or right as it had with her. He'd been in lust before, but never in love until now. He didn't know exactly how it happened, but it did and even he was shocked by his feelings for her. It wasn't shallow or casual or a fleeting passion and as much as he missed his best friend, he had a feeling Kyle would understand because he had loved Mackenzie. She was an incredible woman and he hoped that given time, she would see that what they shared was meant to be and that there was nothing wrong about it. He wouldn't push her and if what she wanted was for them to never cross the line again, he would have to find a way to deal with it. For now, he needed to concentrate on work and getting their new business venture up and running.

"Alright guys, let's get to work," he said, snapping out of his funk.

He was about to join all the moving around when his cell phone buzzed on his hip.

"This is Travis Blackwell," he said, not recognizing the number.

"Travis, it's Commander Shield. I need to speak with you about a private matter that I may need your help with."

"Fellas go ahead and get started, I have a call I need to take in my office."

Trey headed back into his office for some privacy. If his old commander was calling him directly, it was important.

"What can I do for you sir," he asked acknowledging his rank.

"No need for formalities with this. I know you and your team haven't officially started your private investigations company yet, but I have a problem and I need your help. I need some off the record Intel and since Lincoln is the best, I'm asking for your help."

"Anything you need sir, just ask it."

Trey sat down and grabbed a pen and paper and listened as the story unfolded about the identity of an intelligence operative whose identity may have been compromised. He was working on a case in a country where he should not have been and because of the

173

diplomatic chaos that could ensue if he were found out, finding and extracting him without anyone knowing about it was key. He listened and took down everything his commander knew and Trey let him know that he'd be on top of it. His commander let him know that money was no object and that he'd let the highest levels of government know that he was reaching out to Trey and his team because he knew from years of having these same guys under him and carrying out top priority and top secret missions, he knew he could count on them. The commander told him that he'd wire over any monies they would need to get things started and that the payday on this case would be huge as long as they could get him back to the United States safely. This operative had information that was key to protecting the identities of other operatives around the world in hostile environments.

Trey hung up with thoughts of Mackenzie temporarily on hold and he went to get his team ready for their first, yet unexpected mission. They wanted to be game changers and they were about to get their opportunity.

18

Mackenzie sat in the diner waiting for Ava to arrive which gave her time to think through how she would explain ending up at Trey's house after the club and then landing in his bed. She felt relieved knowing that she had someone to vent to and get a different opinion on her night with Trey and what seems to be happening between them.

Even now, thoughts of Trey naked and bulging in all the right places, played havoc with her body. She'd temporarily put all negative thoughts about being with him to the side and she concentrated on the feel of him as he kissed her, touched her and made love to her throughout the night. Her body was on fire for him and every time he entered her body, it was the greatest feeling she'd ever experienced and she remembered the excitement of being with him.

Excitement was the furthest thing from her mind

when she remembered the look on his face right before she walked away. She'd hurt him after she confessed to her thoughts about their time together. She shouldn't have said the things that she did knowing it wasn't his fault that they'd made love nor was it her true feelings. She woke up with so much regret and she lashed out. She wanted him as much as he wanted her and thanks to her decision to come to his house, they'd given in to their desire for each other and it was wonderful.

Her nerves kicked into overdrive the moment she saw Ava walk through the door. She was about to do something she'd been dying to do all day which was to finally tell someone that she'd fallen in love with Trey Blackwell and she was afraid of how it would look if anyone found out.

She waved so that Ava could spot her and took a deep breath the moment she sat down.

"I hope you're starving because the food is great," she said opting to buy herself some time.

"Yeah, yeah skip all that preliminary foolishness. You know why we're here," Ava said grabbing the menu playfully.

The waitress walked up and took their orders and left with nothing else to do, she looked over at Ava who was smiling from ear to ear.

"Okay, spill it and don't you even try leaving anything out," Ava said with a lot of attitude, something Mackenzie had been expecting.

"I don't know where to start," she admitted.

"Well you can start by telling me why you wouldn't

admit to me that you had more than a passing interest in Trey?"

"Whatever I was feeling, I certainly didn't expect to end up in his bed all night long," she admitted."

"Whoa, wait a minute. I know you told me he caused that nice little mark on your neck, but you said nothing about ending up in bed. You had sex with him and didn't call me right after to tell me? I'm starting to question our friendship," she joked, which made Mackenzie smile.

"I've been trying to decipher how it all happened since I woke up this morning in his bed with his arm around me. I was terrified at the feeling that I let my desire lead me to put my friendship with him at risk by crossing a line he and I never should have crossed."

"I won't ask for details because there are some things that even friends need to keep to themselves, but I do want to know how the evening turned out with you in his bed. You can keep everything else after that to yourself," she laughed.

Mackenzie was about to spill the beans when their waitress arrived with their drinks.

"Earlier in the day Trey and I kissed and I mean we really kissed. If I hadn't stopped it, I think we would have had sex then, but we different. Cooler heads prevailed and we walked away. I can't say that happened after I showed up at his house when I left the club last night. My car just sort of went in the direction on its own without any steering from me."

"So when did you decide to jump his bones? Was it

before or after you left the club? Did the two of you plan to leave the club early? You know I noticed he'd left and then you left, but I didn't make the connection last night."

Mackenzie grabbed a napkin to wipe her mouth.

"Leave it to you to be straight and to the point."

"Girl, you didn't meet me yesterday. You know I'm straight to the point with no chaser. Now, I'm trying to figure out how you ended up in his bed."

"I was on my way home and I couldn't stop thinking about that kiss. I took out my phone several times to call him because I didn't want things between us to be strange because of the kiss, but before I knew what I was doing, I steered my car in his direction and ended up in the driveway of his home. I wasn't sure if he was even home since he parks his truck and his car in his garage, but I was already past the no return point. At first I hoped he wouldn't open the door, but when he did, all I saw was a gorgeous man and I wanted him more than I wanted to breathe. That man with no shirt on is like the stuff in those hot, steamy romance novels."

"Kenzie, I'm telling you we need to bottle this stuff up and sell it or better yet, write a romance novel about this stuff. I'm on the edge of my seat anxious for what's next. Now if you're about to jump right into the sex part, yeah you can leave that out."

"No, we didn't just jump right into the sex part. He asked me if everything was okay and I couldn't get a word out. He was standing in his living room after locking the door and when I turned around after getting inside, I failed to notice that when he'd opened the door, he was shirtless and you know how he looks without a shirt.

Remember that day at my in-laws when he was taking the wood off of his truck for their deck rebuild, it was twenty times better than that. The man has the body of a god and I couldn't stop looking at his bare chest. He had on some sweatpants that rode low on his hips and all I could think about was how hard I would have to concentrate to get them to drop to the floor."

Mackenzie started fanning herself.

"Girl, stop fanning yourself. What's happening to you has nothing to do with the heat in this place; that is all you over there all hot and bothered. That man must have really put something on you."

"Understatement of the year," she acknowledged.

"Yeah!" Ava shouted and then covered her mouth when others turned and looked at them.

"Seriously Ava?"

"I'm just saying it's about time. I swear every time I'm in a room with the two of you I feel like we'll all die in a ball of fire because things between you are so hot. So when do you tell everyone that you're involved especially now that I know? I now give you permission to tell others."

"Very funny, but there is no involvement and there is nothing to tell anyone else. It was a mistake and as soon as morning hit, so did my feelings of regret. Trey and I should not have had sex last night because now things are going to be all weird and I pretty much told him, several times that it was a mistake and pretty sure he's pissed off at me."

Ava's stunned look told her everything.

"Why would you do a dumb thing like that after you drove over to his house, went inside and had your way with that incredible body of his? Do I need to give you a course on relationships since you've been out of practice for a while?"

"Again, very funny, but no you don't. I woke up realizing that what we shared wasn't casual; it was more than that and then I realized it couldn't continue. It's Trey, Ava and knowing that, I know it can't lead to anything that wouldn't end up hurting a lot of people?"

"Wait, what people? You can't be talking about you because clearly you got your pipes unclogged last night and it's about time let me tell you. You can't be talking about him because, well, it's Trey and I know he cares about you as more than just a friend. You certainly aren't talking about Kylie who knows a hot, sexy man when she sees him because every time she seems him, her arms go out for him and the way she lays her head on his shoulder is just adorable. I think she actually prefers him over you anyway, but I won't tell anyone. So the only people left who would care are Kyle's parents and his sister and I'd say they would want you to be happy and there is no better guy out her for you than Trey, so what is the problem?"

After the waitress placed their food in front of them, Mackenzie exhaled before diving in to explain her stance on why anything that she or Trey thought could happen after the night they'd spent together couldn't happen.

"First, I agree with you about Kylie and I still don't understand what happened there. I've never, ever seen her take to anyone the way she has with Trey. It's like she knew him even before she met him and it's crazy how she never wants him to put her down when he's around like he's the best thing since breast milk. I thought that would have worn off by now, but no such luck. I don't care who's in the room, as soon as she sees him, he's all she has an interest in."

"True and you should also admit that he loves that little girl like crazy."

"Yeah, there is that too. Now Kyle's parents are another issue. Carmen I can see not being too concerned about it, but I think his parents would see my being with Trey as some kind of betrayal. Suppose they think that Trey and I have had something going on when Kyle was alive? It's only been a year and already I'm in bed with someone and to make matters worse, that someone happens to be Trey. This can't turn out good Ava, it can't."

"Don't do this to yourself Kenzie. Don't let the chance at happiness escape you. You know how quickly life can change so if you find a love that you never thought you'd have again, don't let it get away. You were a mess after Kyle died and I, for one, was scared at how depressed you were. I never thought you'd overcome that and get back to any semblance of

181

normalcy, but you did and a lot of that is due to Trey. He helped you men a broken heart and for that I'm grateful to him. You know I'm going to be on your side no matter what."

"I know and I appreciate that, but I'm still in this dilemma."

"Don't let thoughts of what anyone else will think impact your decision of where you find happiness. I think Kyle's parents love you enough to not assume anything shady was going on and even if they find it strange at first, I think even they'll be able to see that you and Trey have a chance at something good. They know what you went through with losing Kyle and to know that you could be happy again even if it's only been a year, I know it will be okay. Now if what you wanted was to scratch an itch, then fine, move on because now you've done that, but if you know it's more than that and I think it is because I know you and you don't do anything unless you are willing to put your all into it, then go for it and let nothing stop you, especially nothing that resembles regret. Now, stop second guessing yourself and tell me about how you're going to make this right with Trey because I'm not accepting anything else, but that."

Mackenzie tried to think of some witty comeback, but watching Ava devour a jumbo cheeseburger threw her into a fit of laughter.

"Only you can toss out advice while engulfing a greasy cheeseburger. Let's eat, let me think this through for a few days and I'll figure it out. Thanks for the insight and I'm glad I could get it off of my chest. I was dying to tell you, but wasn't sure that I should and now I'm happy I did. You know, I really do like him, but I'm scared."

Mackenzie thought about that and then changed her mind, taking the honest route.

"No, let me change that. I don't just like him, I'm in love with him and yes that scares me."

"I know you're scared and it's okay. Just make sure you give it some serious thought before you say no and walk away from the one man I know can put the broken pieces of your heart back together again, permanently. There is something there so go for it."

Mackenzie smiled and bit into her own sandwich and for the first time all day, she felt good about her night with Trey and terrible for how she made him feel.

19

"Hey Trey, you have a visitor in the lobby," Dustin said coming into his office where he was focusing on the plan to extract an operative from a hostile country.

"Visitor? Who is it?"

"Until we get an office assistant, I'm not taking names and numbers and though I know this person, why don't you get your head out of those papers for a minute and come out to see who it is."

Before he could engage Dustin in comical banter, he disappeared from the doorway. Trey got up to see who would be visiting at their building when not many people knew much about their company yet.

As he reached the lobby, he was surprised to see Mackenzie standing there.

"Mackenzie?" he said

Mackenzie turned around and her stomach did flip flops at just the sight of him. Even though he was fully clothed, she couldn't help it when her mind sent her back to their night together two weeks ago. She hadn't talked to him since that morning.

"Hi Trey."

"Is everything okay?" he asked, surprised because he never expected her to show up out of the blue. The last time she'd done that, they ended up in bed and since the morning after, he had not heard from her though he'd called her several times.

"Yes, everything is okay. I know we haven't talked, but I was wondering how you were and I wanted to drop off your invitation to Kylie's birthday party."

"You know you could have mailed the invitation and if you would have returned any of my calls, you would know how I was doing."

As soon as the words left his mouth, he realized how short and without feeling his words were and he didn't want to be on the defense with her.

"I'm sorry if my stopping by interrupted you," she replied somberly.

Now he felt worse.

"No, I'm sorry. I've been having a stressful day working on a case and it has me a little bit on edge."

"Your company is up and running already?"

"Not really. We're doing something for a friend and it's pretty tricky. Why don't you come back into my office, if you're not in a hurry?"

Mackenzie came all this way to see him and the last thing she wanted to do was turn around and leave. She'd been thinking about him and her need to see him drove her to him.

"No, I'm not in a hurry," she said following him.

"Where's Kylie?" he asked as they entered his office.

"She's with Carmen at a birthday party. A cousin of theirs was having a party and I had errands to run so Carmen offered to take her since she's off tonight. She's then going to drop her off at my in-law's house for the night. I'll pick her up tomorrow evening after my shift."

"Ah, a free few days for you then."

"I'm hoping to get some laundry and a few other things done around the house today because I have a double tomorrow at the hospital. So how are things besides the stress over the case you're working on?"

"Everything is good. We've been busy getting the office up and working on hiring a few people to keep things running smoothly around here."

"I see you've guys have been busy with construction around here."

"Yeah, sorry about the noise. There is a lot going on downstairs. So Kylie is having a party huh?"

"Can you believe she's about to turn one? Time sure is going by fast, but I'm excited about the party."

"I hear she's walking now. I saw your in-laws the other night and they told me you were able to catch her first steps on video."

"Yeah and she surprised me when I saw her standing. I wasn't sure if she was going to take her first steps or drop down to the floor and crawl like she always did. She surprised me and luckily I was able to get my phone out and capture it. Do you want to see?" she asked, happy that their conversation wasn't odd.

"Yeah," he said coming around from the seat at his desk to join her on the sofa along the wall.

"Here it is."

"Wow, look at that. She really is growing fast and look at those little legs go."

"I was wondering if she was going to be walking before her birthday. So do you think you'll make it to the party?"

"I wouldn't miss it. Thanks for inviting me."

Trey looked at her and wondered where the conversation would go next. They couldn't possibly spend the whole time talking about Kylie. Awkward silence hung in the air and to him, Mackenzie looked uncomfortable, but he didn't want to lead the conversation into their night together and waited for her to say what she really came to say.

"I'm sorry Trey."

"Mackenzie, if you came by to tell me that you're sorry we slept together and you regret that night, you've already said that and I heard it loud and clear."

"You really are tense aren't you?"

"I should let you finish."

"I wasn't saying I was sorry for that night because I can't really be sorry for something that was special to me and I know that now. I'm sorry for the things I said to you that morning. At the time I meant them because it was strange and unfamiliar and the only thing I knew to do was to strike out at you for what we did. I've had some time to think about it and I know that there was no fault in any of it. What we did, we did because we

187

both wanted it and I don't want there to be any tension between us. I care about you, clearly Kylie loves you and we're always going to cross paths, so I was hoping we could move past this and get back to where we were."

Trey relaxed glad to hear they wouldn't be getting into another argument. He looked over at her and marveled at her beauty. Even casually dressed she was the sexiest woman he'd ever known and that's saying something considering his past with the ladies. If he had anything to say about it, there would be no other women in his present or future except for Mackenzie.

"Thank you for letting me know and I'd like nothing more than to get back to where you don't ignore my calls," he said smiling to let her know he wasn't being serious.

Mackenzie gazed at him and all she could think about was how great his lips tasted the last time they were together. She had it bad.

"I've missed talking to you and I have no doubt Kylie has missed you. You know I've been trying to figure out some of her baby babble and I think I finally figured out when she says, day-day-day, she's trying to say Trey."

"What?"

"Sometimes when she's playing, she repeats the word day over and over again until the other day I was cleaning and when I laid some pictures on the table from the mantle over the fire place to clean, she picked one up of you and Kyle and repeated da-da-da and day-

day-day over and over. I looked at the picture and when I pointed to you she did it again and I realized she was trying to say your name. I've been teaching her that Kyle was her daddy so I know what she means when she says da, but I couldn't figure out the word day."

"Ah, I got it. That's cute. I miss seeing her too. I've been busy here at the office and I haven't been by your in-laws house to check on them and sometimes I know Kylie is there during the day when you're working. I've missed seeing and talking to you. I know this is crazy, but we need to figure it out. We can't continue on this emotional rollercoaster we've been on lately."

When Mackenzie looked up at him and saw his sincerity, her heart melted into a big blob. She missed him so. She loved the night they had, but she didn't see that happening again if they were going to try and maintain any level of friendship without sex getting in the way.

"I don't know where we go from here when it comes to anything other than friendship between us and I don't want to ruin that, so can we have that night and realize that for the sake of our friendship and those around us that we move forward?"

"I can't say that I'm not going to want you because that would be a lie, but I will respect your wishes. I don't want things to be uncomfortable between us especially around others."

Mackenzie's thoughts were scattered. If she were true to herself, she would admit she didn't want things to go back to what they were. She wanted something more, but her problem was she didn't know what.

"I know and we will. Anytime you are missing Kylie, feel free to stop by. You know you're always welcome."

Mackenzie stood and walked over to the door with Trey following close behind her, almost too close. She could smell the rugged, sandalwood scent of his cologne and he smelled amazing. Combined with his sexiness, she'd be in trouble if she didn't soon leave. She paused when her hand reached the handle of the closed office door. The moment Trey's hand covered her, she shivered from the contact and heat fused between where their hands met. Adding to the allure, she could feel his hot breath on the back of her neck.

"What about if I'm missing you? Is that invitation to come by still an open one?" Trey spoke on a whisper directly into her ear causing the little hairs to flutter. Damn, her reaction to him was insane.

Trey was standing close enough to feel her shiver and it made him smile. She can try to fight what's happening between them if she wanted, but he wasn't going to make it easy for her. He didn't want to push, but he couldn't shake the fact that they were making a huge mistake not taking a chance on what they could have.

"Trey," Mackenzie said on a sigh.

"I know, but I want you to think about something besides us going back to being friends by your definition. If I promise to take things very slow, would you consider having dinner with me sometime?"

"Slow?" she asked. "You're pretty good at slow."

That slipped out of her mouth when what she wanted to do was say it in her mind.

You're being an enchantress even when you're not trying to be. I'm sure you didn't mean for me to hear that, but I did. Don't hide from me Kenzie. Anything you want or need from me at any time, you only have to ask and in response to your statement, yes, I'm good at slow, fast or any other speed I need to be at, remember?" he said saucily.

"You're going to make this hard for me aren't you?" she asked on a whimper.

"You are not the only one this is hard on."

Trey chuckled lightly and tried not to smile at the double entendre because being this close to her, he was hard as a rock.

"I see I have to watch my words around you," she chuckled.

"Turn around," he pleaded.

Mackenzie turned around and came face to face with him.

"Dinner Kenzie."

Trey's voice was deep and gruff while at the same time she heard a bit of mischievous that told her dinner could mean a variety of things. To her, those two words sounded provocative showing that she wasn't the only enchanting one.

"Dinner?" she asked

Trey chuckled again. She was losing the battle against fighting her attraction to him.

"Yes, just dinner Mackenzie, unless you tell me

otherwise."

"Okay, just dinner. When?"

"Tonight? You're free, I'm free."

"Okay, dinner tonight. Where do you want me to meet you?"

"For starters are you okay with someplace local or would you like to drive a bit? I'm not trying to hide the fact that we're going out together. I'm thinking about you. I don't want you spending the entire evening looking around to see who's watching."

Was she really that bad? Yes she was and it was her own fault.

"Someplace different would be nice and I don't mind a drive."

Mackenzie hoped her attempt to get some distance between them and Monterey wasn't too obvious. They were only having dinner and since they were friends, it wouldn't be out of the ordinary, but deep down, she knew that there was nothing about the two of them that truly was just friends.

"Are you sure you don't want me to pick you up or you can meet me at my house and I can drive?"

"No, I have some things I need to do first and it would be easier for me to meet you there."

"Okay, I have a spot I've heard about out in Pacific Grove. Is that too far or far enough?"

"That's fine."

"Then I'll see you tonight."

Mackenzie turned to leave again and this time Trey stopped her from turning away from him. Before she could weigh what he was going to say or do, she moved closer without thinking when she saw his six-foot-three frame lean down with his eyes glued to her lips. Without thinking, she stuck her tongue out to moisten her lips and before she retrieved it, Trey leaned down and captured her tongue between his teeth and planted a searing kiss on her that had her entire body tingling. The kiss didn't last long, but it left a powerful impression, one that left her breathless and wanting more.

Trey released her sooner than she wanted him to and stepped.

She felt hypnotized as she watched him slowly lick the essence of her from the kiss from his lips. It was the most erotic thing she'd ever seen.

"Whew. Just dinner right?" he asked hoping that at least one of them would be able to control themselves.

Mackenzie couldn't part her lips to say anything afraid the feel of his lips on hers would disappear. After several minutes of working to get her body back in check, her mind cleared up enough for her to finally respond.

"Just dinner Trey and I'm going to leave before anything else happens. Clearly we can't seem to keep our hands off of each other."

Trey couldn't agree more. His mind was already playing out a scenario where he saw himself swiping everything from his desk to the floor in order to strip her of every stitch of clothing and giving into the desire that was engulfing them. The magnitude of the insatiable lust they have for each other was evident to him even if she continued to deny it. For now, he'll let her continue to process what he knows is inevitable. He exhaled and pulled back.

"I'll walk you out."

Mackenzie stopped him with her hand.

"I think you need to stay right where you are and let me find my way out. Our goodbyes don't seem to turn into real goodbyes at the door and you need to wipe the lipstick from your lips before you go back out there."

"Do I have to? I like the taste of you there," he said glibly.

Mackenzie laughed.

"You can't resist being irresistible can you?"

"I don't know. Is it working? It only matter if it works on you."

She shook her head at him and smiled.

"Wipe the lipstick off Trey. Unless you've had other women in this office today that you've kissed, I think the guys may be able to put two and two together."

"Dustin is the only one still here and he already knows about us. The other guys are probably gone to a scheduled meeting offsite."

Mackenzie's head snapped up, not sure she heard him correctly.

"Wait, did you just say Dustin knows about us? What does he know Trey?" she said nervously.

Trey regretted the admission the moment shock hit her face. He couldn't get out of explaining even if he wanted to.

"I'm sorry Kenzie, but yeah, Dustin knows. I was struggling with this thing between us and I explained everything to him to see if I was losing my mind being interested in you."

"Oh my goodness. I can't believe you did that."

Trey saw her getting riled up and calmed her.

"Anything I've said to him was done in the strictest confidence. He would never tell a sole and he won't judge either. Trust me when I tell you, if I thought otherwise, I never would have said anything."

Where she was about to get upset, Mackenzie pulled back because he had done exactly what she had; told someone in order to vent, so she couldn't blame him. She had an admission herself.

"I told Ava. What did Dustin say?"

"He said he saw nothing wrong with it as long as you and me could deal with it, we shouldn't worry about anyone else. What did Ava say?"

"Pretty much the exact same thing."

"Yet, here were are still questioning it," he said.

Trey was right, but she didn't want to talk about it right now. She smiled to let him know everything was okay.

"I'll see you tonight."

Trey grinned and waved knowing that tonight was going to be the beginning for them. He needed to get her on board.

20

Mackenzie walked nervously up to the entrance to the restaurant. She knew Trey was there after seeing his truck on the parking lot. It took her a little longer to find it. If it wasn't for her focusing on being cautious, they wouldn't have had to come all the way out to Pacific Grove to have dinner together.

She went up to the hostess, gave her name and was escorted to the table where Trey sat. He stood when she reached him and came around to give her a hug. She expected another kiss like the one earlier in the day, but instead he leaned down and planted a soft kiss on her cheek.

"How did you find this place?" she asked after he sat down.

"I asked Dustin and he said this place was out of the way and had great food."

"Dustin. Right because Dustin knows."

"It's okay Mackenzie. I trust Dustin with my life. Believe me, I can trust him with everything else."

"I know and it's okay."

"You look beautiful. I don't see you with your hair up often and I like it."

Mackenzie reached up to her hair as if to straighten it. He was right, but tonight she felt like doing something different with it.

"Thank you. Having this much hair and with as thick as it is, it can get pretty tricky sometimes and it's easier to just pin it up."

"Trust me when I tell you, you could have come in here in a sack and cornrows and you'd still be the loveliest woman in here."

Mackenzie smiled and picked up the menu.

"Everything sounds great. I think I'm going to have the broiled fish special."

"I'm going for a steak. I have always been a steak and potato kind of guy."

"I do remember that about you."

After placing their order they settled in for idle conversation which soon turned to their current predicament; where do they go from here.

"So is this considered a date?" she asked.

"Yes, it's a date and I hope it's the first of many, though I'm hoping we won't have to play mission impossible to find out of the way places."

"We both agreed to this," she explained.

"I did this for you, not for me. I don't care where we go as long as I get to be with you. I want to be with you

Kenzie and if that means I have to do this in a way that won't have you running away from me, then so be it."

Mackenzie looked at his face and saw how sincere he was. He was making every effort to consider her first in this and here she was still hesitant.

"Trey, I don't want you to think that I spend my day trying to come up with more ways to avoid you, blame you or convince you that this can't go anywhere. I also don't want you to think that what you are feeling is a one-way street because it isn't."

"I know it's not, but I think that we aren't on the same street and together in this. If giving us a try is not what you want, then say that, but we are playing a constant cat and mouse game and in the end, it will hurt us both because when we should be honest, we're not."

Trey was right. She was playing around the outside of the field, but not diving into the game with everything she had.

"You want some truth?"

Trey smiled. "I want all of the truth and trust me, I can handle it."

Here's everything, she thought.

"With everything that's in me I want to be with you. I may be struggling and fighting my feelings, but they are true and I know what I want and that is you. Honestly I wonder the impact it will have on Kyle's family more than anything. How would they react? I think if it didn't go over well, you would be the one cast to the side because I have Kylie and they love her. I

198

don't want to see anything come between the love you have for them and they for you. Don't you understand I am trying to protect you here; I don't want to see you hurt."

"Kenzie, I don't need you to look out for me because I'm a big boy."

"Yes you are," she exclaimed and then covered her mouth. One day she'll learn how to think something without saying it out loud.

Trey caught on and when he looked over at her, they both laughed so hard that people around them turned to see what was so funny.

"Remarks like that are why I had crazy thoughts of stripping you naked in my office today. I know you want me. It's evident every time I look in your eyes. I see that want staring back at me and it's not a casual or fleeting want either. There is more here than that one night we spent together. If we put that on the side for now and took things slow, giving you time to see that our coming together is okay, I would take and I'm willing to wait as long as you want me to wait."

Mackenzie exhaled as she stared into the eyes of a man who was putting his heart on the line and putting it in her hands. It was up to her what she decided to do with it. She was about to speak when the waiter showed up with their order.

Conversation ceased for a moment as they ate, giving them time to figure out what to do next.

"I don't want to walk away from you Trey. I didn't think I'm ever come out of the funk I was in for almost a year, yet there you were, being that solid rock friend that I needed. I can't imagine making it through without you. I agree that there is something between us that is unexpected and despite what may eventually happen, I don't want to go back to a time when I can't sit across from you like this and feel as comfortable as I do now. I don't want to hold back any part of myself from you."

She looked at him as she spoke looking for any reaction and she saw none. She saw that he was giving her his undivided attention.

"You know how I feel and I'm already there."

"I have one request Trey and it's non-negotiable."

Trey put his fork down wondering what he would have to agree to.

"What's that?"

"No telling anyone else. I'm not ready for anyone else to know until we figure out if this is something we both know we are going to want beyond where we are right now. I need to know that this isn't something that has come out of a loss we both suffered through."

He could deal with that.

"I won't share anything about us with anyone else, but I don't think we should wait too long before we tell the Ellis' and Carmen. I think we're setting ourselves up for something bad if we keep this from them and somehow they find out."

"I know what you mean and for now, let's just see where we're going and I'll know when it's time for me to tell them about us."

Trey smiled when he heard her refer to them as 'us'.

"I see this makes you happy," she said.

"It makes me happy to hear you consider you and I an 'us'."

"I did say that didn't I?"

"Yes you did and I like it. It gives me hope that you're not afraid to see us that way."

"I'm not afraid."

"That's good to know."

Now that the weight of what was next for them was over and they would figure it out without any more reservation, Trey was happy when they settled in to enjoy their official first date.

After an hour of talking about Kylie, her work at the hospital and his work at Game Changers, Mackenzie let out a yawn and laughed at how embarrassed she was. She didn't want Trey to think that he was boring her.

"Tired a little? This reminds me of the many nights of talking to you to help you fall asleep. I never thought it would happen with me sitting right across from you. I guess it's time for you to get home since we have a drive ahead of us."

"No Trey, I'm sorry. I'm not tired at all and I'm not ready to go home yet."

He looked at her questionably. If she was tired, he didn't want her driving home tired.

"Are you sure?"

"Yes, I'm sure. I'm having a good time with you."

"Are you up for a little drive?"

"Drive where?"

"There is a remote spot that overlooks the ocean that I want to show you. It's not too far from here. We can go in my truck and leave yours here on the lot until we get back. I'm not ready for you to go yet either."

Trey reached across the table and took her hands in his. She heat from his eyes and his hands turned the temperature in the restaurant. She was more than ready to leave and spend some quiet time with him, hopefully in his arms.

"I'm ready whenever you are."

Trey paid the bill and hey walked to his truck.

21

"This view is incredible!"

"I knew you'd like it," Trey said reaching across the seat and taking her hand in his.

"I'd like to come back here in the daylight. I bet it's even more beautiful."

"We can come here and go any other place you'd like any time you want. All you have to do is say so."

When Mackenzie turned toward him and their eyes met, Trey knew that there was nothing in the world that could keep them apart and he was going to make sure that she never hurt again.

"I'm glad we came out tonight and thank you for giving us a chance. I know you're taking a risk, but I know everything will work out fine in the end," he said.

Mackenzie had to believe him because for the first time in a long time, she doesn't feel like the weight of the world is on her shoulders and her heart was definitely on the mend.

"I wish these seats weren't separated by this section

in the middle," Mackenzie said pointing to the large cup holder in between them.

"Come here," Trey said reaching for her.

Mackenzie moved in his direction without second guessing herself. Trey slid his seat back so that she could sit in his lap and they could enjoy the skyline overlooking the ocean together.

After sliding over into his lap, she leaned her head back on his shoulder and didn't like that she couldn't see him. She shuffled around until she no straddled his lap and they were face to face.

"I know we've only had that one night together, but I've missed being this close to you."

"I've missed you, too."

Mackenzie couldn't resist when his penetrating stare drew her in and feeling like a large magnet was pushing her closer to him, she leaned forward and while never taking her eyes off of his, she kissed him softly on the lips. She felt Trey return the kiss, but to her surprise, he let her control the moment. She reached up and rubbed her hands across the stubble growing on his chin, something he could now grow since he was out of the military. Wanting more from the kiss, she linked her fingers behind his head and when he parted his lips slightly, she took that as an invitation to take the kiss deeper and she did.

Trey thought any minute, his hard erection would push through the seam of his zipper in order to get close to Mackenzie. He wanted her with a fierceness, but he knew this wasn't the place for them to indulge.

He needed a bed.

"I know we decided to take it slow, but there is so much a brother can handle. My will power doesn't go as far as it should and not far at all when it comes to you. Given the fact that you're sitting in my lap and there's only a clothing barrier keeping me from being inside of you, we're playing a dangerous game sweetheart."

Mackenzie moaned, but didn't speak. She wasn't trying to let will-power control her. Right now she wanted him and truck or bed, she didn't care. All she knew was she needed to feel him inside of her before she took her next breath.

Showing him that she could be just as aggressive as him, Mackenzie reached between them and stroked his huge arousal through his pants. She heard and felt his intake of breath the moment her hand came in contact with him.

"You do realize we are sitting in my truck where anyone could walk by and see us."

"Trey, we are in the middle of nowhere. If anyone is out walking around spying on us, then they were meant to do so and in a few minutes, they're about to get a show," Mackenzie said smiling and letting him know she had no plans to stop.

"You are a dangerous woman."

"You haven't seen anything yet."

Mackenzie, not getting the feel she really wanted, unbuckled his belt, undid the snap and reached for the zipper taking great caution as she unzipped his pants knowing how hard he already was. She didn't think she would ever tire of how aroused he gets when they are together.

"You are so hard and from what I remember from our first night together, you stay hard and ready."

"Apparently I have to in order to keep up with you. Who knew you had this wild side. You have me sitting in my own car with my pants unzipped and wondering what can I do to pleasure you next. You bring out the animal in me," he admitted.

"Well mister animal, please tell me you have protection with you."

"I do, in my wallet. You'll have to lean up some in order for me to get to it when you're ready for it."

"I'm ready for it now!"

Trey laughed out loud.

"I am to please," he said.

"If my memory serves me correctly, yes you do."

As he retrieved the protection, Mackenzie made herself more comfortable on his lap. When he was about to cover himself, she reached for the condom.

"Let me," she said breathlessly.

With shaky hands, she covered his hardened flesh while stroking it at the same time causing him to grow longer and harder in her hands.

"You are one beautiful man and I mean every single part of you."

After getting protection in place, Mackenzie squirmed on his lap trying to get closer to him as he leaned forward placing open mouth kisses across her neck and finding just the right spot to bite and suck.

"You taste and smell wonderfully," he admitted.

"Yeah, well it's your version of tasting me that got me in trouble with Ava. She saw a mark you left on my neck after that night together and she quizzed me until I told her."

Trey sat up and looked her in the eyes.

"Ah, so that's how she found out."

"I had to tell her because she knew it had to be someone. I tried lying and that didn't work at all. I've never lied to her and I knew she could keep a secret. I was nervous that she'd find something wrong with it, but she didn't. She wanted to know why I was having such a problem with it. Our secret is safe with her."

"Baby, I don't care who knows. The only person I'm worried about is you so that this isn't uncomfortable for you especially when it comes to anyone else finding out."

"Trey, I don't want anyone else to find out. I'm still coming to grips with what we're doing and I need some time before anyone else finds out."

"Well, I did tell Dustin, but that was because I was miserable after we had the argument the morning after and I was making life around the office a living hell. Believe me he won't tell anyone and neither will I. This is our secret for now until we can find out what this all means. For now, I love making love to you in a bed, here in my truck and anywhere else I can get inside of you and speaking of that," he said looking down to the area where he couldn't wait to join their bodies together.

Thankful that he opted for this large truck and shifting his weight so that they were both comfortable Trey reached down and moved the thin strip of her panties to the side and holding on to her firm behind with his free hand, he lifted her up slightly and in one long swoop, he pushed up into her body just as she came down on him which made them both gasp at the pure please of them coming together again.

Mackenzie's mouth opened while her eyes closed at the exhilarating feel of him as he eased his member inside of her one delicious inch after the other. She wanted to concentrate on nothing, but the feeling.

"Don't close your eyes. Look at me baby," Trey whispered through clinched teeth.

When she opened them and their eyes locked, Trey was a goner and knew that he never wanted to let her go.

He watched her as she rose and fell adding a swivel to her hips, making him plant his feet firmly on the bed of the truck to brace them. She was a beautiful sight to behold as she rode out her pleasure, not taking her eyes off of him. The feel of her was so great that without thinking about it, he slowly closed his eyes to concentrate on the feel of her wrapped around his member so tightly. He felt her using her inner muscles to tighten and then loosen her grip on his penis and he popped his eyes back open to look at her in the moonlight.

"What are you doing to me," he grunted trying to hold on, waiting for her to get her pleasure first.

"Keep your eyes on me and you'll be able to see everything I'm doing."

Mackenzie took their love making to the next level by leaning back and placing her hands on his knees and riding him as if she were riding a real stallion. She loved that the only sounds to be heard were of their heavy breathing and moaning and the wet sound of their bodies slapping against each other.

Trey's eyes were glued to her actions and watching her was a delight in itself, besides the feeling of her writhing around in his arms. The vision of her body bouncing on his and her breasts doing their own dance in his face, he used one hand to reach into the top of her dress, pulling it down until her breasts were exposed for his pleasure. Holding her tight, he sucked one nipple into his mouth while using his hand to caress the other large globe. He rolled the nipple around in his mouth savoring it and pulling on it lightly with his teeth.

The moment Trey began sucking on her breast, she knew she wouldn't last much longer. Mackenzie reached up and gripped his head, holding it in place as she rode him harder and faster until the tension in her body built up to the inevitable explosion that tore through her without pretense. She closed her eyes as streaks of lightning streaked across her eyelids while her body consumed stroke after stroke until she could no longer contain the feeling. Her screams of pleasure pierced the dark night sounding like an animal in heat in the woods.

Seconds after Mackenzie's orgasm had consumed her, Trey bellowed louder than any roaring lion as his body shook with wave after wave of pleasure which overtook him. He tried to control his actions, remembering that Mackenzie was astride him. He continued to surge up into her until their breathing calmed and Mackenzie fell forward, slumping in his arms.

Trey caressed her back as her body calmed from their passionate love making.

"Mackenzie, are you okay?" he whispered in her ear.

She had not moved for several minutes, choosing to lay in an exhaustive lump against his chest.

Trey could barely move himself after what they'd just experienced. He'd been with a lot of women in his life, but nothing matched what he and Mackenzie experienced this time or the first time. Their coming together was out of this world.

"Mm, hmm," was all Mackenzie could get out. She didn't want to move and couldn't form her mouth to actually say any words. She wanted to stay like this with him, intimately connected.

"Baby, are you uncomfortable sitting like this?"

"I've never felt better and at the moment, I'm not even sure I have legs anymore," she joked.

"Well if you don't, I know for a fact that it's for a good reason. Lean up and look at me."

After she leaned back, Trey took her face in his hands and kissed her and not just a small peck, but a deep intoxicating kiss that was meant to remind her that he was in this with her.

Trey wasn't one to lay all of his cards out on the table, but the fact that he and Mackenzie were giving themselves a chance at happiness together, he wanted her to know how he really felt about her. To him, there would be no more holding back.

"I love you Kenzie."

Mackenzie didn't know how to react. She knew she loved him too, but she didn't know how to handle the feeling. Was it wrong to be in love with him? Were they living in a secret fantasy world that they could actually be in love and it would be okay with the people around them? They wouldn't be able to keep loving each other away from those who loved them both. She never thought that there would be room in her heart ever again to love anyone in an intimate way, but here she was in love with Trey and he'd just told her he loved her. She didn't want him to think he was in this love thing alone.

"I love you too Trey and I'm scared. I'm not scared of my love for you or your love for me, but of our love for each other. What are we supposed to do at this point? We can't forever have this secret love and I know it, but I don't know how to love you in secret; I don't want to, but I feel like I have no choice."

"Kenzie, for right now, I'm willing to settle for this love just between me and you. I know you've struggled a long time with a broken heart and I don't want you to forget that feeling of love in your past because it's a part of where you and I are today. I don't want this thing between us to overwhelm you to the point that it pushes you away from me. I didn't plan this just as you didn't, but now that we are here, I want to live in this moment until we figure out what to do next."

"What next is what scares me the most. I won't say that we haven't thought about the repercussions of our coming together because I think we've both thought about it in our own way. I'm not so sure it won't hurt others around us who won't understand. I'm not quite sure I understand how we ended up here, but I will say that I don't regret it. I questioned myself after that first night with you, but I don't want to anymore because I know that I deserve to have love and happiness in my life and I was a total basket case for so long and that wasn't healthy for Kylie. The question is, what's next?" she asked hoping Trey could provide some insight.

"I want to have the answer for you, but I don't have it. The only thing I know is that we were brought together at a time when we both were grieving and out of that came our love. Though it's unexpected, I won't deny it and neither should you. I think we could have something special once we figure out how to do this and not hurt those around us. To be truthful, I think if we handle this right, I think they'll understand that we didn't set out to fall in love, but love is what brought us together."

Mackenzie shook her head in agreement.

"Look, we don't have to solve the problems of the world around us tonight. We had a great time at dinner and you made sure we had an incredible, yet unexpected time just now and what I want to do most is get you back to a bed and wake up with you in my arms in the morning. While Kylie is with the Ellis', this is the perfect time for me to hold you and love you through the night and tomorrow, we'll look at our situation with open eyes and clearer heads. Right now, my head is filled with thoughts of you and getting you completely naked."

Mackenzie smiled.

"I'm ready when you are," she said sliding off of his lap and adjusting her clothes.

Trey adjusted his own clothes and looked around. He didn't see anyone lurking around and was thankful for the very darkly tinted windows on his truck.

"We better get out of here before someone finally comes by after hearing the animal sounds that we emitted from the car," he laughed.

"Yeah, you with the king of the jungle lion roar probably woke up every animal in the woods. Now they're probably mating like crazy too."

"Then we better leave them to it and find a place to do our own mating. Let's first get you back to your car and let's go to my house. This time, Kenzie, with no regrets."

"No regrets," she agreed.

**

Carmen waited in the car outside of the restaurant while her boyfriend Lance grabbed carryout meals. She was glad to finally have a night off from the hospital and when he asked her to take a drive with him just to

213

take in the California night, she jumped at the chance.

They ended up in Pacific Grove, one of her favorite cities along the coast. When they decided to head home, Lance found a restaurant on their way back to Monterey where they could order takeout to eat once they returned to his house for the night. She was glad he decided to leave the top down on his Mercedes because the sky was beautiful.

She was about to lay the seat back while waiting and out of the corner of her eye, she saw a truck pull into the parking lot not far from where she sat. What caught her eye about it was that it was a custom made truck that she recognized. Carmen wondered why that truck would be so far away from Monterey. She guessed she wasn't the only one on a road trip. She was about to get out to go over and say hello when she saw Trey exit the truck, go around to the other side and when the woman exited, she sat straight up in her seat.

What the hell? Why were Trey and Mackenzie together? Perhaps they were meeting friends she thought. She sat still and watched what occurred next that had to have been some kind of dream.

Carmen watched as Trey walked Mackenzie over to her car parked a few cars down from where he pulled in. There was something in the way they were looking at each other that bothered her. This wasn't a friend greeting or conversing with another friend; this was two people who were in a world that included just the two of them. They had eyes only for each other.

"No way," she said out loud, not sure she was

believing what her eyes were seeing.

What happened next put her in danger of having a heart attack.

Trey pulled Mackenzie to him and Carmen watched as they leaned into each other and kissed. It wasn't just a simple kiss, but a passionate one that's shared between lovers. It went on and on and Carmen was all set to go over to ask them what they were doing together and kissing.

"This can't be happening."

"What can't be happening?"

She jumped at the sudden reappearance of Lance. She didn't want to bring him into what she saw.

"Oh, nothing. I was thinking about something, but it's nothing."

She played it off and out of the corner of her eye, she watched Mackenzie get in her car and pull off, followed by Trey. She would confront the two of them later. There is no way she'd be able to let go of what she'd seen and she wanted to know how long it had been going on. For now, she let it go and focused on her own night.

"Are you chilly? Do you want me to close the top on the car?"

"No, I'm fine. What did you get for us to eat?"

"I got a big variety of things. Let's head back to my house."

Carmen shook her head and they drove off in the same direction that she'd seen Mackenzie and Trey go in.

22

"Someone is having a good day today," Trey heard as he strolled through the office.

Trey shook his head and kept walking.

"You have something to say when I'm grouchy and now you have a comment when I'm in a good mood. Can I walk into this office and be ignored like everyone else?" he jested.

Dustin got up and followed him to his office.

"I would ask the reason for all this happiness we've seen from you for the past week, but unbeknownst to the other guys, I think I already know. Things are good huh?"

Trey smiled.

"Things are better than good; they are great."

"So you and Mackenzie have worked things out? Are you telling people yet because the guys know something is up with you, always rushing out of here to meet a mysterious woman and not telling them anything? You know we've always shared our conquests in the past, but only because I know this isn't your typical conquest have I not said anything."

"I appreciate that. We've decided to not say anything to anyone else for now, not sure how her in-laws and other friends would take it."

"You know sooner or later they'll figure something out and you don't want them to find out without you telling them."

"I know, but I'm playing this by her rules. I don't want this to cause any kind of problems so for now, until we figure out what we have, we see each other when we can."

"I can't believe that the greatest at being a playboy that I know has fallen in love."

"Surprised the hell out of me too, especially knowing it's Kenzie. I tried to fight it until I no longer could and now we're spending time together when we can until we've figured it out."

"Isn't Kylie's birthday party this weekend?"

"Yeah, are you still coming by?"

"Of course. That's Kyle's little angel and I wouldn't miss it for the world. I hope I won't have to referee romantic looks between you and Mackenzie the whole time. Since I know, I'll see things others won't see so cut it out for those few hours."

"Yeah, yeah, whatever. I got you, no sexy glances at her from across the room. Got it," he quipped.

"Man, I'm just glad to see you smiling. There has

been a lot going on lately and with the business that will be coming our way, I need your head in the game."

"I hear you and I'm on it. How is everything coming with the below ground construction?"

"We've tried to keep most of that work to the evening hours, especially the weapons and equipment deliveries. There is some pretty powerful stuff coming in and all that equipment for the underground situation room is incredible. I don't know how you were able to get your hands on some of that stuff. I understand our government doesn't have a lot of this stuff yet."

"There are those at the highest level of command in the military who know what we are trying to do here and are looking forward to our help with cases where the United States can't get involved. We have the capability and the men to pull off missions that will be seamless and will work in collaboratively with the work they can do in the light of day. Game Changers, will be the first of its kind. Next week we'll be meeting with military and non-military men who will become a part of the team. Our country needs this and our cover will be the security services and private investigations we'll do which is the public scope of our work that we're releasing to everyone. The situation room will be key in keeping track of what's going on across the world."

"This is good work, Trey. I left a few of the resumes for the additional interviews for you to go through."

"I'll get to them later on at home. Right now, I need to see my woman," he smiled.

"Oh, you being all in love is so sickening," Dustin chided.

"One day when the love bug hits you, you'll understand."

"Never, my brother. That's never happening to me. There are too many woman who count on me to keep them satisfied for me to give all that up for one woman."

"Never say never," Trey said before grabbing his phone to call Mackenzie as Dustin left.

"Hey!" Trey said when Mackenzie answered.

"Hey yourself."

"I know you're working a double tonight, but I was hoping I could stop by and see you on my way home. I've missed you since you've been working this crazy overnight schedule the past few days."

"I miss you too. Things are pretty slow today and I have a break soon if you want to come by the hospital."

"Are you sure you're comfortable with that? Is Carmen or Ava on duty?"

"Neither of them are working today."

"Good. I'll grab some food and I'm on my way."

"Okay, come in through the emergency entrance and I'll make sure I tell the guard to escort you to my office. We can relax there until I have to get back out on the floor."

**

"This is the first time I've been in your office. So this is how they treat their best doctors, huh? This office is bigger than some houses I've been in."

"I lucked out and got this office when I came back."

Trey looked over at the small bed in the corner of the office. He got an idea, stood and walked over to it.

"Just how comfortable is this bed? Is it comfortable enough and quiet enough to do anything other than sleep?"

Mackenzie caught on quick when she saw the lust-filled look on his face.

The idea frightened and enticed her. Spontaneous love making in her office could be dangerous since neither of them know how to contain the sounds of pleasure that escapes when they're in the throes of passion.

"Trey, we can't."

"Why not. I'm actually feeling a little tired and would love to take a moment to lay here and you know what would make it even better? If the most beautiful woman I know in the world would join me."

Mackenzie stood unable to resist the heated stare from across the room. She'd never been as uninhibited as she was whenever she was around him. She turned out the lights, checked to be sure the door was locked and joined him in what she knew would be an afternoon delight for her.

**

"Hi Trey."

Trey, startled to hear his name called turned around and came face to face with Carmen as he walked toward his car in the hospital parking garage.

"Carmen, hey," he stuttered out.

"Fancy seeing you here."

"Yeah," was all he said. He didn't want to lie and he couldn't think of an explanation.

"Yeah? That's it? Let me help you out a little bit. How about, yeah, I was just visiting Mackenzie who is more than just the friend that you and your family have thought we were all this time. Am I close to anything?" she said calmly, tampering down her anger.

Carmen knew.

"I'm sorry does a cat have your tongue or did you lose it in Mackenzie's mouth?" she said angrily.

"Whoa, wait Carmen, it's not what you think."

"Really what am I thinking? Before you tell me let me tell you that it's not a good idea to devour my brother's wife in the parking lot of a restaurant. I saw the two of you. What the hell was that and how long has that been going on? Before or after Kyle died?"

Shocked to hear her insinuation, all bets of avoiding the truth were off the table.

"Carmen, nothing was going on until recently. This isn't something casual nor was it planned. We grew to care about each other having leaned on each other through everything. I'm in love with her."

Trey braced himself for Carmen's rage.

"What? Love? When? How?"

"Okay, calm down and let me explain."

"Yeah, you better," she replied. This was Trey, someone she considered a brother and she couldn't get the image of him and Mackenzie kissing out of her head.

Trey took his time and explained everything to Carmen, leaving out any intimate details. He wanted her to know that what he and Mackenzie were engaging in was not planned and it wasn't casual. Neither of them expected to go beyond friendship, but they did and it was out of mutual love and respect; not something dirty and demented. He started explaining from the beginning with the phone calls when Mackenzie was in Virginia.

Thirty minutes later they were still standing in the same spot. Trey appreciated that she let him lay it all out for her without interrupting and she appeared to be softening following his explanation.

"Mackenzie loves you too?"

"Yes, Carmen she does, but she's afraid of what you and your parents would think. I promise you nothing ever happened between Kenzie and I before no. It may have started out that we grew closer because of our grief over Kyle, but it grew to more than that and as much as I would like to say I fought it, I'd be lying. You know me and you know that I've never been in love before and I've never told a woman I was in love with her, so you have to know that this is real for me. It's also real for Mackenzie, but I won't speak for her. We have been discussing how to tell everyone and hoped that you would all understand that our falling in love wasn't something we jumped into lightly. It's been a struggle understanding what falling in love would mean for us and all of you and especially Kylie."

"Trey, I know that you wouldn't lie to me and I know

222

that you wouldn't do anything to hurt any of us. When I saw the two of you kissing, nothing mattered except that I saw you two kissing. It never dawned on me that the two of you would have been drawn together and the result would be that you've found love with each other. I can't say I understand it fully, but I will say that I don't find anything wrong with it. I think Mackenzie is a great person and you already know that I think the world of you and Kyle is not here anymore. He would want you both to move beyond grieving and to get on with your lives. None of us would have ever imagined that you would move on together, but love is love, right?"

Trey breathed a sigh of relief.

"Are you sure you're okay with this?"

To show Trey that she was, Carmen reached up and gave him a hug.

"I swear this isn't weird at all. I just needed to know that this wasn't something from long ago and I believe you when you say it wasn't. What happens now? Are you going to tell my parents about this? Don't let them find out the way that I did. They need to know."

Trey has been struggling with that same assessment all week. He'd stopped by their house earlier in the week and he didn't like keeping something this big from them.

"I've wanted to tell them for a while. It's Mackenzie who is hesitant."

"Mackenzie loves my parents and I know she doesn't want to hurt them. I don't think this will. I think if you explain it to them the way you explained it to me, they would understand. They loved Kyle and they love you and Mackenzie. I'm not sure Mackenzie will ever be up to telling them. Perhaps you can talk to them and pave the way for her to be open with them about this."

"I don't know Carmen. That seems a lot like going behind her back."

"I understand Trey, but if I know Kenzie, she's never going to work up the nerve to and I can't keep this from them. I don't like secrets and they deserve to know. If you really love Kenzie, don't continue hiding this. Do what you need to do and talk to them and if Kenzie loves you, she will understand why you felt you needed to get this out. I promise I won't say anything to Mackenzie, but that only lasts for today. After today, I will have to say something to her about what I saw and I think it will crush her to know that I saw the two of you before she had a chance to tell me and my parents about it. I've already held on to this for a week."

"Thanks for the support Carmen. It means everything to me."

"You and Kenzie mean everything to me and I'm glad that you found each other. I couldn't have picked a better person for her to fall in love with than you."

Trey gave her one last hug and jumped in his car. He left the parking garage and turned in the direction of Kyle's parents' home. It was time.

23

Mackenzie walked into her in-laws house and knew that something had changed the minute she saw everyone's attention center on her. She didn't get the usual happy greeting she got when she showed up to pick up Kylie. She looked from face to face from her father-in-law, to her mother-in-law, then to Carmen and then finally, standing near the fireplace with a look on his face as if he was about to face a firing squad was Trey. This can't be good, she thought.

"What's wrong?" she asked of everyone.

No one responded as they looked quizzically at each other. Her first thought was that something was wrong with Kylie, especially when she didn't see her. She grabbed her chest in fear.

"Where's Kylie?"

"Kylie is fine Kenzie. She's asleep in the back

bedroom," Carmen said.

"So nothing is wrong yet everyone is looking like they've seen a ghost."

Mackenzie came further into the room and still no one moved and all eyes stayed on her.

"We, uh, were talking to Trey and Carmen about a few things."

She turned to her mother-in-law and knew what they were talking about.

"Were you? What are those few things you were talking about," she said, turning to look directly at Trey making sure her eyes questioned what she knew he shared with them.

"You've been seeing each other and it's been going on for a while? Suffice it to say we're quite shocked to hear that. I mean, I've seen some passing glances between the two of you, but I had no idea you've been seeing each other, dating and sleeping together? You walked in at the exact moment where Trey was telling us what was going on. To also hear that Carmen knew and no one said anything to us is a little hard to take in right now."

Mackenzie turned to her mother in-law, not sure what to say in response. She didn't have time to prepare for the encounter. She then turned her anger back around to Trey.

"What did you tell them? Why would you tell them? I asked you, I begged you to let me tell them. I knew this would happen and this is what I wanted to avoid."

"Kenzie?"

Mackenzie heard her mother-in-law call her name, but kept her focus squarely on Trey.

"Why would you come over here and hurt them this way? I don't understand why you couldn't keep this to yourself like we talked about until I was ready to deal with this and explain things to them."

"I didn't come here to hurt them or you. I came here to talk to them because the secrecy was killing me and it was going to kill us."

"Look at them Trey? They are hurt and it doesn't take a genius to see that. This is my family and the one thing I wanted to avoid was this very scene right here. I knew getting involved with you was a huge mistake and I don't know what I was thinking. I knew it was wrong and I let myself get caught up knowing the situation could ruin my family."

Trey was hurt seeing how much pain she was in. He didn't want this.

"Mackenzie, let me explain."

She stopped him from saying anything additional and turned away from him and back to her in-laws to explain.

"I am so sorry for this and I know I've betrayed your memory of Kyle and getting involved with Trey was a huge mistake. I have no excuse for my behavior since I know you consider him another son. I'm sorry for hurting you like this and if I have to beg you for the rest of my life to forgive me, I will do it," she pleaded through the tears that were streaming down her face.

"Being involved with me was a mistake?" Trey asked

sadly from behind her.

Hearing the words were like having a knife stabbing him over and over again. He was further crushed when she didn't turn back around to face him, but spoke with her back to him.

"This isn't about you or me Trey, it's about the pain we're causing them by our actions. Can you leave so that I can talk to them please?"

"No, Mackenzie, I'm not leaving and I think we can all talk this out."

"You've done enough talking. I can never forgive you for this and I never want to see you again."

Mackenzie did turn to him then and if her stare could turn him to stone, he'd be a pillar. She started crying uncontrollably and Carmen came over to give her support.

"Perhaps you should leave Trey and let us talk to Kenzie."

Trey turned to Mr. Ellis and without saying a word walked out of the house.

"Why don't the two of you go check on Kylie and let Kenzie and I talk," Darleen said.

When there was only the two of them left, Kenzie turned away in shame. How was she going to be able to look them in the face again knowing that every time they saw her, they would be seeing her with Trey, their dead son's best friend?

"Kenzie, come sit down."

Mackenzie didn't move and kept her back to her mother-in-law.

"Mackenzie, come sit down."

She did turn then and still not making eye contact, went to sit next to her.

"I'm not sure what to say here other than I need you to turn around, look at me and tell me how you really feel about Trey. I don't want you to say what you think I want to hear or what you think would satisfy any of us; I want to hear from you what this is between the two of you."

"How could I have been so stupid to get involved with him? I don't know what happened and I don't have an excuse."

"Kenzie, I'm not asking you for an excuse; I'm asking you to tell me what's going on and what has been going on?"

Mackenzie gathered herself and prepared to beg for forgiveness.

"I don't know when it happened, but I found myself seeing him different and not just a friend. I promise nothing ever happened while Kyle was alive. I never considered him as anything more than a friend, but a few months ago my feelings for him turned into more than just friends and I think I let my loneliness and broken-heart lead me to him. I know there are lots of other men around and I don't know why it ended up being Trey."

"Are you in love with him?"

Mackenzie didn't answer, afraid of the hurt her response would cause. She was madly in love with him and angry at him at the same time. She'd hadn't felt this alive in a long time and she knew it was because Trey set out to mend her broken heart and he did that. As a result, she saw him as the only other man that loved her as much as Kyle had. She couldn't admit to her feelings for him and at the same time betray the love she has for Kyle.

"I don't know," she replied softly.

"Look at me Kenzie."

She looked up and unexpectedly she didn't see the look of an angry or hurt mother. She didn't see judgement or disappointment, but what she thought she saw was understanding.

"You caused a scene and threw Trey out of our house and you didn't need to do all of that. Listen, I love my son and I will forever love him and I love you and Kylie just as much and no matter what happens, that will never, ever change either. I also love Trey like a son and he's been here for David and I since Kyle died. I know that if the tables were turned and Trey had died instead of Kyle, Kyle would be in Florida right now looking after Trey's mother because that's how close those two were. Don't you dare be ashamed for loving Trey and deep down I believe that Kyle would understand and Pop and I certainly do. I will admit we were shocked to hear it and when you came in, Trey had been explaining things to us. What you saw was not anger or hurt, but it was our initial reaction to hearing it. Trey told us that you both tried to fight the attraction between the two of you, but I don't understand why you would. You are a wonderful woman and an incredible mother to our only grandbaby. Trey is one of the finest young men we know and if anyone in this world is going to treat you and Kylie with love, I know it would be him. You can't help who you fall in love with as long as no one is getting hurt in the process and in this case, no one is. Well no one except Trey since you kindly threw him out."

When Darleen smiled, Kenzie smiled back. She had blown things out of control.

"You mean you're not upset about this?"

"The only thing I'm upset about is the fact that you felt like you couldn't come and talk to me about this, but instead hid it like it was a dirty little secret when it's far from that. Now I'm going to ask you again, are you in love with Trey and I want you to be honest with me."

"Yes," she admitted without hesitation.

"That's good because that boy loves you and the look on his face just now when you asked him to leave was heart-wrenching. The look on his face when you made him feel like he meant nothing to you is one I never want to see again. I'm going to go in the back to play with my granddaughter whom I can hear is wide awake now and I think you need to go and talk to Trey. Kyle is gone and I know he would want you to find love again and the fact that it's with Trey doesn't lessen your love and devotion to Kyle and his memory. Life is too short to have two broken hearts in one lifetime, so don't let that happen. We are your family and we love you and Trey and Kylie wouldn't be happy if she didn't get the chance to see him again. There is nothing bad about the two of you falling in love other than if you don't get out of here and fix things with him, the bad part will be that you have a second chance at love and you let it walk out the door."

Mackenzie wiped her tears, gave her mother-in-law a hug and ran for the door in search of Trey. She was all prepared to check his home and office in order to track him down to apologize. She reached for her cell phone while rushing to her car and dialed his number. She was just about to jump in her car when she heard his line ringing in her phone and then a phone rang close by her. She looked up to see that he had not left, but was standing against the side of his truck looking at her smiling.

"You're still here!"

"I told you from the beginning that I wasn't going anywhere and I don't give up that easy. I saw that you needed a moment with your family so I gave you that, but I had no intentions of leaving here without first talking this out with you and with them. I figured I'd give you guys about thirty minutes and then I was going back in that house."

She didn't care what made him stick around because all she knew was that she was happy to see him. Without warning, she ran at him full speed, dropping her purse and her phone right before leaping into his arms. No more words were needed as their lips met in a titillating and ravenous kiss. Mackenzie kissed him with everything she had in her when knowing that she almost walked away from a love some women don't get to experience once in a lifetime and she had it twice.

She held on tight with her arms wrapped around his neck as he held her tight in his embrace. He wasn't mad at her and he didn't let her harsh words deter him from staying put and fighting for their love.

"I love you!" she said when she pulled back from his lips.

"I love you too. What changed your mind?"

"Darleen chastised me for letting love slip through my fingers a second time. She understood that you sometimes can't help who you fall in love with even in a circumstance like ours."

"I love you, baby and loving you as much as I do can't be wrong and I wasn't ready to let you make me think that it was. It was the right time to tell them about. I don't want to rush anything with us, but at least now, we don't have to hide away like a dirty little secret and you can now feel better about us."

"Darleen said the same thing and couldn't believe we have hidden what we have from them."

"It was wrong for us to do that, but not wrong for us to fall in love. I know you came to pick up Kylie, but before you got here and all hell broke loose, they were talking about a barbecue. All this sneaking around works up a brother's appetite," he joked.

Mackenzie kissed him again before putting her feet back on the ground.

"Thank you for loving me."

"I told you that if you gave me a chance, I would un-break that broken heart of yours. I don't want us to ever forget about Kyle, but I know he's smiling knowing that I've done everything in my power to make sure that you didn't mourn forever and that you got back to living your life. Thank you for letting me love you."

Epilogue

Mackenzie's phone range as she entered her in-law's house with Trey in tow. She looked at it and saw Ava's number. She couldn't wait to tell her that she and Trey no longer had to hide the fact that they were in love. She told Trey to go ahead of her while she talked to Ava. He needed to get the barbecue started.

"Girl, where are you? We need to talk," she said grinning as if Ava could actually see her.

"I need your help."

Mackenzie stopped in her tracks when she heard the solemn tone in Ava's voice.

"What's wrong?"

"It's my sister."

"Sister? You have a sister?"

"Yes and she's in grave danger and I don't know what to do. I think someone's coming after me."

"Calm down Ava and tell me what's going on."

"I can't right at this moment. I have to get out of the hospital, but I don't know where to go. I think someone is coming to kill me."

Mackenzie could hear her sounds of breathlessness that told her she was running and out of breath.

"Where are you?"

"I'm running down the steps of the hospital to get to my car in the garage."

"Trey!" Mackenzie hollered in the house.

In seconds Trey was standing next to her and his smile turned to a frown when he saw the frightened look on her face.

"What's wrong baby?"

"Something is wrong with Ava. She said someone is after her to kill her."

Trey took the phone from her.

"Ava, it's Trey. What's going on and where are you?"

"I'm at the hospital trying to get out of here. I can't explain everything at this moment, but I don't have anyone to turn to besides Kenzie. Please help me!" she pleaded.

"Stay here at the house Mackenzie and I'll bring back your phone," Trey said racing to his truck.

"Ava, I'm not far from the hospital. Stay on the line with me and do everything I say. Is this threat to you already in the hospital?"

"I think so, but I'm not sure. I just know that I need to run and get out of here."

"Okay, is there any place you can hide out of sight where no one will see you, not even people who know

236

you, until someone gets there? If you're running and someone is looking for you, they will probably assume you were headed for your car so don't go there."

"The old wing of the hospital is closed off and no one goes in there."

"Is there a way out from that part of the hospital without going back into the main part of the hospital? Perhaps a door of any kind that doesn't lead out to the main street?"

Trey hopped in his truck and was now speeding in the direction of the hospital while dialing Dustin on the phone in his truck.

"Yes, the door to the old morgue entrance backs into a loading dock and it can't be seen from the street or the main hospital."

"Go there and make sure your phone is on silent, but watch the screen. You will either get a call from me or from Dustin. He read Dustin's number off to her. As soon as you hear back from either his number or Mackenzie's number because I have her phone, I want you to smash that phone into pieces with anything you can find. Now, hang up and go there, find a place to hide until you hear from one of us."

"I'm scared Trey."

He could hear the fear in her voice.

"I know and we're on our way, but I need you to calm down enough to get to a safe place. We'll be there soon."

He hung up just as Dustin picked up the line.

"D, where are you?"

"Heading over to the hospital. We have a game changer situation."

"Is it Kenzie?" Dustin asked.

"No, it's her friend Ava and it sounds serious and dangerous. I need you already on your way there. Take her number because she'll be expecting a call from you. I told her to destroy it as soon as she hears from you or me with further instructions. She's going to be in the old wing of the hospital, you know the area that's closed off? She said there's a loading area where the morgue was that's hidden from the street. If you get there before me, extract her and get her back to the safe room at the office."

"I'm on it."

Trey hung up and raced to get to the hospital. He knew that all he needed to say was game changer and his team members knew that it was time to jump into action. He didn't know what was going on with Ava, but he could hear the genuine fear in her voice and if someone was out to get her, he knew that he and Dustin needed to get there first and get her out. Game changers had their first on the book case and he was ready for it.

*Join Cheryl Barton in the release of the first installation of her first fiction crime novel, **Game Changers: On the Lam**, available in paperback and for your e-pub device in August 2016.*

*Introducing **Heartthrob**, a romance novel by Cheryl Barton, now available in paperback and downloadable for your e-pub device*

"Mr. Weston, can I get a moment of your time?" a voice shouted.

"Cade! Over here please," another voice bellowed in the crowd.

"Cade, what was the most challenging aspect of your most recent film?" a male shouted over all the other voices.

"What do you like most about being Cade Weston, being an actor, running your own record label, having a successful apparel line or is it the countless number of women who throw themselves at you daily?" a female voice shrieked.

"Cade, can I have your baby?"

That question made him laugh, something else he heard daily.

"Mr. Weston, what's next for you, is it a new movie or a brand new business venture?" another voice hollered.

"Mr. Weston, are you single? I have a daughter and I think she'd be perfect for you!"

Cade smiled as questions were being thrown at him from the crowd that gathered outside of the Los Angeles television station. It was daytime, but he had just wrapped up the taping of his appearance on a late night talk show. He was told to expect the crowd once word got out that he would be there. He expected a crowd, but nothing like what he encountered as he exited the building while his team of security made a path so that he could get into the waiting limousine.

"Cade, what do you think of the nickname everyone has given you, calling you 'Heartthrob'? I hear it's because of the number of broken hearts you leave behind and the throbbing bodies women and some men experience just by getting a glimpse of you?" yet another voice shouted.

Cade stopped in his tracks at hearing himself being called heartthrob.

Recently, that pseudonym had been plastered on the cover of every magazine and news story written about him. He liked it, especially when people tried to define the title with their own characterization. He found it hilarious each time he read a new story about him and his sexual prowess, something that kept his name in the headlines.

"You don't have time to stop and answer questions Cade," Abby, his personal assistant said, urging him to keep walking.

Cade knew she was right and though he was tempted to answer some of the questions, he continued on to the limousine and got in followed by Abby and Aaron, his chief of security.

"That is some crowd, especially this early in the morning," Aaron said.

Aaron was not only Cade's chief of security, but also one of his best friends since their college days.

"It is and I am who I am because of crowds like

that."

"I see this heartthrob thing isn't going away. I'm beginning to think you're enjoying the title, brother."

Cade didn't answer, but gave his friend a slick smile. Being labeled a heartthrob and plastered on the cover of magazines certainly had its benefits.

"What's on the agenda for today?" Aaron asked.

"I'm going home to work out and then I believe I have several meetings at the record label. My artists are climbing the charts and because of that, we've been getting in demos from aspiring artists from around the world. There are a few my team who is responsible for new talent want me to hear. Then, later tonight, I'm going to be eye candy on the arm of Ms. Diamond at a fundraising event. Does that about cover it Abby?" he asked turning toward her and making sure he hadn't left anything out. He noticed she had yet to lift her head from her cell phone no doubt booking him for another public appearance somewhere. He didn't question her; he just followed along.

"That's pretty much it. You asked me to clear your calendar after the event with Ms. Diamond tonight."

Aaron knew what that meant. Cade was often called on to accompany some of the most beautiful women in the world to events to keep the buzz about them in the media. He knew that Cade believed that all press was good press in Hollywood. He had, after all, recently been name the sexiest man on the planet. Everyone wanted to be seen with him and all women wanted to get under him, literally. Aaron had a feeling Diamond would be engaging in both before the evening was over.

"Abby, can you get my usual suite ready for tonight and since I'll be entertaining, roll out the usual including my staple gift. Check to be sure it's not one that I've given Diamond in the past."

"Do you want me to add flowers this time as well?" she inquired.

Cade thought about it and knew it wouldn't be necessary with Diamond.

"No flowers tonight, but make sure my driver sticks around since she won't be staying all night."

Abby didn't respond or even react since they were all accustomed to Cade's penchant for entertaining and then moving on. This was going to be one of those nights. He would be doing his part to keep Diamond in the spotlight by being seen with her and in turn, she would spend the evening in whatever way he chose. He was Cade Weston, media mogul, box office smash, actor and of course, according to the entertainment world, 'heartthrob' and he planned on living up to that name tonight.

*Enjoy this excerpt from **Amorous Occupations: The Dancer** by Cheryl Barton – Now available in paperback and downloadable for your e-pub device*

Max tried to remain calm as the dancer came toward him in the seedy New York night club where he knew no one would recognize him. He was sure his dark attire and the baseball cap sitting low on his head that partially covered his face shielded his identity from anyone who wasn't standing directly in front of him.

He never thought he'd be in a place like this where men came who needed relief from their home lives which consisted of wives and children who placed demands and pressures on them daily. He had neither a wife nor children, but tonight the darkened club with a dozen or so sexy women clambering about trying to entice men and women out of their hard earned money all for a few lap dances, provided the fantasy he needed to do what he came to the club to do.

Max watched several women as they gyrated around the club going from one hand that held out money to the next, hoping to entice a few into something a little more personable. Unbeknownst to them, he wasn't there to get a lap dance. He had other plans in mind for the dancer who was slowly making her way over to him. He'd been trying for several nights to get her attention and had high hopes that tonight would be the night that she'd tune into the signal that he was interested.

As the music played loudly and the liquor poured non-stop, Max sipped on his beer and waited. He didn't have to wait too long once the dancer made eye contact. When he didn't look away, he assumed she thought she had him. Little did she know, she was the one being had.

When she finally reached him, he remained calm, but the rapid tapping of his right foot told another story. He looked at how she was dressed in a hot pink thong, very high heeled clear stilettos and nothing else. He looked at her breasts and could see that she wasn't a very voluptuous woman, but her shape was perfect for him and for how he needed her to look. The familiarity was perfect.

Max let his eyes travel up and down her body as she sashayed around for him making sure he could see her from every angle. When she turned around, showing him her backside, his heart skipped a beat. Now that her face was turned away from him, in his mind he could imagine her looking like anyone he wanted and when the face of the woman he wanted her to be flashed before his eyes, his body jumped with anticipation.

Tonight was finally the night, he thought to himself. He could barely contain his excitement over how the night could turn out. Now that the sexy little vixen was finally about to give him some attention, he knew that his patience had paid off. As she turned back around to face him, coming right up to him he knew it would be the perfect night, at least for him. This time was a long time coming from when he first began his search for the right woman. Max knew she had to be perfect and after not getting the joy and excitement from the first few women he lured in, he had a feeling this one was what he'd been looking for.

Max had come to this place several times, scoping it out. His first visit was to check out the place and to see if any of the women looked like his Shelly. He'd been to several places like this one around the city in hopes that one would resemble the love of his life. An unwavering exhilaration resonated throughout his body the moment he spotted her on his first visit.

The dancer looked so much like his Shelly that they could pass for twins. As the days went by, Max knew that she may be able to pass for Shelly in the looks department, but her dance moves were not up to the standard of Shelly's, who was a professional Broadway actress and dancer. Tonight that fact didn't matter much to him since it wasn't her dancing skills he was interested in.

Steadying his legs as she came up to him became a task as she leaned over so that her naked breasts were mere inches away from his face. Not wanting his nervousness to scare her away, he never took his eyes off of her face, giving her an even, intense stare. It was her face that became the draw and the obsession for him. She had the same beautiful, flawless face as Shelly, though she wore more makeup than he liked. Her long weaved hair flowed down around her shoulders in a cascade of loose curls that he couldn't wait to grasp tightly in his hands. If he thought it wouldn't draw attention to them, he would reach for her now, but he needed to wait. The time for that was getting closer.

"You're watching me," she said in a soft, sultry voice.

Max's body stood at attention.

"Since you came up to me, I assume my watching you intrigued you," he responded.

He was hoping they wouldn't waste a lot of time conversing because he knew it would draw attention from others in the club to them, something he didn't want.

"Well, what will it be tonight handsome?" she asked.

"Not something I can get sitting here."

When she didn't immediately respond, he knew she was thinking about what was obviously a subtle proposition.

"Where would this something you'd like to get need to take place?"

"Well sweetness, it depends on you and what time you get off."

"Well, I'm not really allowed to leave with the customers; it's against club policy."

Max went in for the kill to make sure she changed her mind.

"Well I have a thousand dollars that says your club policy is null and void tonight."

The mention of that much money got her attention when he saw how wide her eyes widened.

"You have a place near here big spender?"

"Not real close by but I have a car that can get us to my place in no time at all and have you back here at the club in time for your stage time in two hours," he replied calmly, not giving away his anxiety.

"How do you know I have stage time in two hours?" she asked.

"I've been coming here for a few nights and you always have the twelve-thirty a.m. time slot for your show. Right now it's only ten and I can guarantee you that I'll have you where you belong by your show time. I'm so riled up for you sugar that I'm sure things will happen quicker than I'd like, but as soon as you need. What do you say to that? Is a thousand incentive enough for you?"

Max knew he was pushing, but if he didn't make his move tonight, he wasn't sure he'd get another chance. He could see her running the options through her mind, contemplating what she could do with the thousand dollars. He was sure from looking at the clientele, that she'd never make that much money from one customer and in this case, she wouldn't have to split it with the club.

"I could get in trouble and even lose my job if the boss knew I was leaving with a customer, especially one that may spend money in the club tonight."

Max had the answer.

"I'll tell you what I'll do because I really want to spend a little alone time with you. I'll head on out of here, making sure I'm not seen, while you go make an excuse of some type of an emergency, telling your boss you'll be back in a couple of hours just in time for your show. I'm sure you can persuade him to see things your way," Max said, making sure he looked her over from head to toe, letting her know that he meant for her to use her femininity to get her boss to go along with it.

"If I do this, how do I know you actually have this thousand dollars?"

Without any hesitation, Max reached into the inside pocket of his jacket and pulled out a stack of one hundred dollar bills. What he didn't let her see was that only the first five bills were hundreds, while the others were one's, but she was so focused on the hundreds on top and how thick the stack was, that she didn't question him further. He didn't show the money too long, afraid she might catch on so he quickly placed the bills back in his pocket.

"Proof enough for you?" he asked.

"What kind of car do you drive?"

"It's a black Mercedes. I'll pull around the corner so that no one coming in or out of the club will see you get in it. I'll be in it ready to drive off as soon as you get in."

The pull of a thousand dollars for an hour or so with a customer was too big of a take for her to turn down and Max knew it.

"Give me twenty minutes," she said before turning and walking away.

Max got up, pulled his cap further down on his head to block any view of his face and exited the club. Once outside, he wasted no time getting behind the wheel of the Mercedes he'd stolen a few hours ago from a hospital garage. He'd watched the doctor as he showed up for work knowing it would be hours until the doctor's shift ended before he noticed the car was gone. By then, he wouldn't have a need for it anymore.

ABOUT THE AUTHOR

Cheryl Barton lives in Maryland and in her spare time she loves to read espionage novels, cook, watch Sci-fi movies, spend time with family and friends and enjoy Maryland steamed crabs.

Find more books by this author at www.amazon.com/author/cherylbarton